UNDERCOVER BOYFRIEND

BROTHERHOOD PROTECTORS WORLD - GUARDIAN AGENCY

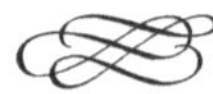

REGAN BLACK

*As always, with special thanks to Elle James for inviting
me into her world of
Brotherhood Protectors.
And for Mark, my personal hero every single day.*

BROTHERHOOD PROTECTORS

ORIGINAL SERIES BY ELLE JAMES

Brotherhood Protectors Series
Montana SEAL (#1)
Bride Protector SEAL (#2)
Montana D-Force (#3)
Cowboy D-Force (#4)
Montana Ranger (#5)
Montana Dog Soldier (#6)
Montana SEAL Daddy (#7)
Montana Ranger's Wedding Vow (#8)
Montana SEAL Undercover Daddy (#9)
Cape Cod SEAL Rescue (#10)
Montana SEAL Friendly Fire (#11)
Montana SEAL's Mail-Order Bride (#12)
SEAL Justice (#13)
Ranger Creed (#14)
Delta Force Rescue (#15)
Dog Days of Christmas (#16)
Montana Rescue (#17)
Montana Ranger Returns (#18)
Hot SEAL Salty Dog (SEALs in Paradise)
Hot SEAL Hawaiian Nights (SEALs in Paradise)
Hot SEAL Bachelor Party (SEALs in Paradise)

Visit ReganBlack.com for a full list of books,
excerpts, and upcoming release dates.
For free reads, exclusive prizes, and much more,
subscribe to Regan's monthly newsletter.

CHAPTER 1

SLOAN MATHISON SIPPED on a tall mug of piping hot coffee and admired the stunning view. A wispy fog drifted across the deep blue water of the still lake. By noon, the surface, as smooth as glass, would offer a perfect reflection of the sky above. Over the peaks of the mountains in the east, the sun was still only a hint of hopeful color on the horizon.

"This makes it easier to understand what you were thinking when you made this move," she said to her brother, Seth.

"Hush. You'll scare off the fish," he scolded with a smile.

It was an argument they'd been having since their first fishing trip over two decades ago. At thirty, Seth was the oldest, but she liked to think she'd done almost as much living in her twenty-seven years. He'd followed the family expectations and joined the Navy, eventually becoming a decorated SEAL. To her father's lingering disappointment, Sloan had chosen a different path, taking a civilian approach to a career of serving others. He'd been so convinced she would be an asset to the Navy as an officer. That wasn't her idea of a good time. Five years into her career as a physical therapist at the VA clinic, her father had almost come to terms with it.

One of the fishing poles arched and Seth stood up to reel in the catch. "Feels big enough," he said, working the line. The short fight was over quickly and he grumbled. "Gone."

Smothering a laugh, she made sympathetic noises. She watched him closely as he baited the hook and cast it back into the lake. Seth had struggled for a year to rehab a shoulder injury. To her expert eye, he was back to one hundred percent, with full range of motion and balanced strength. The Navy disagreed, insisting Seth was no longer fit for duty with the SEAL teams.

Seth wasn't ready to hang up his skills in favor of a desk job. He'd reviewed his options and made a decision in record time. When he'd told Sloan about being recruited to a private security group, she'd only been surprised by the Montana location. They'd been raised on one coast or another through the years. Personally, she couldn't imagine living this far inland. The lakes and rivers were gorgeous, but she *needed* the ocean waves as much as oxygen.

Over the past several days, she'd met Hank Patterson and many of the men and women Seth would work with as part of the Brotherhood Protectors team. So far, she liked them all. Everyone involved demonstrated integrity, loyalty, kindness, and sincere camaraderie. She was certain Seth would fit right in.

A former SEAL himself, Hank understood the transitions her brother was going through. If and when Seth hit any speedbumps on the road between military and civilian life, he'd have support. It made her feel better about being so far away from him.

"You know, I assumed you'd find your new career in California," she mused.

"Aww, will you miss me?"

She rolled her eyes. "No." They both knew she meant yes. That was both the problem and the perk of being close siblings. "Your new boss is really generous," she said, changing the subject with zero finesse. When Hank had heard the two of them sharing stories about their fishing trips as kids, he suggested they come out to this lakeside cabin for the last two days of her vacation.

Seth chuckled. "Everyone says he's the best."

The sun cast a soft, golden glow over the trees and water. Filling her lungs with the bracing morning air, Sloan deliberately steered her mind away from anything beyond this lake, this moment.

Any trouble waiting for her back home in Oceanside, California wouldn't be solved by worrying away the last of this special time with her brother. She hadn't seen him, hadn't spent any real time with him in nearly two years. His service and her career had kept them apart. She intended to savor every minute of this break.

He rolled his shoulders and checked the poles. Apparently, they hadn't found the most appetizing bait for the fish this morning. "I'm hungry." He stretched his arms overhead. Dropping them, he patted his flat stomach.

"That's not news." She poked him in the chest.

"You can solve that problem since you're on breakfast duty."

"Yeah, yeah." He glanced back at the water. "Don't let anything worth keeping get away."

"In other words, *don't* follow your example."

With a snort, he moved past her and headed up the path to the cabin. "I'll be back."

Of course he would. The Mathison family were imminently reliable. It was part of the genetic code, according to their mother.

Alone, Sloan soaked up the peacefulness of the quiet morning. With the stillness came the deep sense of calm she usually only found when she was out in the ocean waiting for the next good wave.

This complete relaxation was such a treat for her mind and body. Now that Seth lived here, she should make a point of visiting more often. She hadn't realized all the raw beauty and natural treasures Montana had to offer.

Her phone hummed in her pocket, startling her. She thought this pocket of heaven was out of range. Had been counting on the respite of being out of contact for a bit longer.

The text message from a coworker scrolling across her screen made her groan.

Making sure you haven't been eaten by a bear.

As if she couldn't take care of herself. The guy would *not* quit pressing her to be more than professional associates. Montana was an hour ahead of California and it seemed ridiculously early for an attempt at banter.

Another message came through before she could delete the first one. This text offered a ride home from the airport. Why wouldn't he give up already? She'd been clear that she wasn't interested in dating. Not him or anyone else.

She was giving serious thought to tossing the device into the lake. Not much of a solution unless she opted for a new cell phone number. She pushed a hand through her hair. Dwelling on the inconvenience of *that* would wreck the morning.

"Trouble?" Seth asked from behind her.

Crap. She hadn't even heard her brother on the path. Turning around, she gave him a bright smile and focused on the platter in his hand. "Breakfast burritos? They smell amazing."

"Good." He set the tray on the table between two Adirondack chairs. "Come here and eat up. Then you can tell me who the troublemaker is."

She took a seat and ate slowly. Refilling her coffee mug from the thermos, she stalled for as long as possible. Involving Seth wouldn't fix anything. Peter Driscoll was a decent guy. Just because he was wrong for her didn't mean she wanted or needed her brother to intervene.

"Come on, Sloan," Seth began. "Talk to me."

"It's nothing."

Seth's eyebrows shot up. "Agree to disagree. Whoever it is has been pestering you the entire week."

"Pestering is a strong word," she argued.

"It's also the *right* word."

"I appreciate the support," she said, treading carefully. "This isn't a big deal." When she got back, she'd remind Peter, *again*, that she wasn't ready to dive back into the dating scene. One heartbreak was more than enough for her lifetime, thank you very much. Although her family believed her lingering heartbreak would heal, Sloan had decided love wasn't in the cards for her. Last year she'd made a deliberate choice that her family, her close circle of good friends, and her work made for a full, satisfying life.

She had zero desire to let love crush her all over again.

Her phone buzzed again and Seth scowled. "Let me talk to him."

"Stop." She jerked the phone out of his reach. "This is the clinic."

Though it was odd for them to call at this hour. As a physical therapist, her patient schedule was firmly set within regular business hours Monday through Friday.

"You're on vacation," her brother grumbled the reminder as she answered the call.

"Hello." No one replied. "Hello?" She repeated herself twice more, to no avail.

"Give me that." Seth made another grab for her phone.

She dodged him easily, then noticed the call ended. "Must've been some fluke technology deal."

"Right." Seth's expression turned stormy. "Basic logic says the pest works with you."

She rolled her eyes. "You've got that whole mission-ready look on your face, but this isn't a crisis."

"It's more than nothing."

Her phone chimed with another incoming text and she powered it off without even looking at the message. "There. Vacation mode activated. Let's check the fishing poles."

"The Brotherhood Protectors have resources," Seth said. "Let me help."

"No," she said firmly. "Thank you."

"Sloan."

"I mean it, Seth. There's nothing to help with. You're reading too much into this."

"Fine." He held up his hands in surrender. "I'll back off on one condition."

"Just one?"

He ignored the jab. "If it escalates, promise me you'll ask for help."

She relented. His heart was in the right place and he only wanted what was best for her. "I promise." And she meant it. If this situation with Peter became a true problem, she would seek out help. Being independent didn't mean being foolish. Still, asking for help didn't necessarily equate to calling in a team of former elite warriors. They were way overqualified for a simple case of pest control.

She'd always valued being raised in a Navy family. She loved her parents and brother, was grateful the four of them remained close. Their concern for her was rooted in love.

But there were times when she wondered why they couldn't seem to reconcile that she was an *adult.* An independent, capable woman utilizing all she'd been taught and building a good life on her own. That included her ability to deal with a persistent man who wanted more than friendship. True, Peter made her uncomfortable, but that didn't mean she'd give in to his doggedness or give him hope when there wasn't any reason for it.

She'd be a broken record and tell him no as many times as it took for him to get the message.

As the sun climbed overhead, Sloan focused on the fishing, changing the conversation toward more comfortable topics, namely how he planned to adapt to the area and which of his friends would come up for a visit first. Though they were used to going months between visits, it was hard knowing his *home* would be over a thousand miles away from hers.

Her line started running and she worked with the fish, following Seth's tips and eventually landing it. After checking the size and taking a picture, she freed the hook and released the fish again. First fish honors went to her, but by the time they packed up for the day, he'd caught three more than she had.

"I could go back with you," Seth offered a few hours later. "Hank would give me the time off and whoever this pest is, he'd definitely get the message."

They were sitting together at the fire pit making s'mores for dessert. She pulled her marshmallow away from the heat before it could scorch and sandwiched it between the graham crackers and chocolate.

"No need," she assured him. "Just focus on you and the new gig for a while. You deserve to take the time and settle in. Maybe find someone special."

He choked on his s'more and she smiled to herself.

Going the day with her phone off had given her time to process the situation in the back of her mind. She'd go back home, clearly state her position one last time and then block Peter's number. That way she'd never even see the texts or voicemails begging her to meet for coffee or anything else.

"I know you can handle yourself," Seth said, circling back to the topic she thought was closed. "Just like you know how big brothers work."

"*Mm-hm*. At this point, doesn't that just make you old?" she teased. "I mean, I'm all grown up and you're *older* than me. It's simple math."

"You're a smart ass."

"Lessons I also learned from you." She gave his

shoulder a soft shove. "I can take care of myself." She ignored the tiny voice in the back of her head questioning her assertion. One way or another, Peter would *not* continue to be a problem. If she absolutely had to do it, she'd report his unwelcome tenacity to the Human Resources department.

"You know who it is, don't you?" Seth asked.

No sense lying. "Sure. He's harmless, just supremely annoying."

"If that changes, you'll call me?" Seth pressed.

"I already promised I would. Please stop worrying. You'll wreck my sugar high." She stuffed a big bite of the treat into her mouth.

"Okay, okay."

He mimicked her, somehow fitting an entire square into his mouth. Some things never changed. They laughed like a couple of loons and her world seemed to click back into place.

CHAPTER 2

JAKE WELCH STEPPED BACK from the heavy bag and wiped the sweat from his eyes. He'd pushed himself hard through an extended workout and still couldn't escape that lingering sense of failure.

Anniversaries sucked. This one more than most.

Three years ago today, he'd lost two of his Delta Force brothers, two of the finest men around, on an op that was doomed from the start. Someone up the food chain had hemmed and hawed too long, and by the time the order had come down to return fire, it was too late to save them all.

Today was a day for distractions and this was the best he could do under the circumstances. His

Guardian Agency bosses knew about the significance of this day and made sure he wasn't on assignment. Jake would consider it an insult, but deep down he knew it was the right call. Better for everyone if he spent the day alone.

Well, nearly alone.

He'd come to the gym for the quickest path to exhaustion so his mind couldn't dwell in the painful past. In addition to the regulars, he'd spotted the tail his bosses had assigned to keep him out of trouble.

Jake smiled to himself as he peeled away the protective padding wrapped around his hands. Gamble and Swann didn't take any chances, not with their clients or their personnel. It was one aspect he appreciated above all others since signing on with the exclusive protection agency.

They'd pulled him from the brink of disaster when he'd returned home to California and gone on a vigilante tear. A rash of vandalism and robbery had put business owners in his hometown on edge and Jake, still trying to acclimate to life as a civilian, waded boldly into the fray. He studied the news reports, asked the right questions in the worst neighborhoods, and eventually picked up the trail.

But he hadn't given the information to the police. No. He'd taken it upon himself to dish out justice. Systematically, the thugs were stopped and trussed up for the cops to find.

Naturally, the police weren't thrilled about his method of assistance. He'd been too cocky, too wrung out with grief to care about being caught in the act of cleaning up the situation. The arrest hadn't come as much of a surprise. He wasn't ashamed of his actions, even in the face of legal consequences. In some ways, Jake welcomed the arrest, the fallout, even the prospect of jail time as the penance he deserved.

When Nolan Swann had walked into the dingy interrogation room and declared himself Jake's lawyer, he hadn't argued. Something in the man's stern expression had given him an incongruous flicker of hope.

Back then, he hadn't known he'd had any hope left in him.

That brief, intense conversation took him from the brink of arrest to a new career with an excellent salary and benefits based in Chicago. Plus, the support and resources of a team that knew how to give the right help without crossing the wrong lines. All they asked of him was to channel his passion for protecting others into the selective, discreet cases of the Guardian Agency.

From day one, it was clear that Gamble, Swann, and their entire agency knew how to get things done. Jake had been challenged, he'd made a few friends, and above all, his efforts consistently contributed to the outstanding success rate of the agency as a whole.

He was once again part of something bigger, part of a team with a clear vision. And, barring sucky anniversary days, he felt like he was operating at his peak once more.

Hearing his cell phone chime from the pocket of his gym bag, he paused just long enough to blot the sweat from his face and down some water before he checked the device.

A single word glowed on the screen: Protect

For a second, he could only stare. He wasn't sure what to think or feel. Should he be elated to have the distraction or worried that they'd called the wrong guy? No one trusted his judgement on this particular day. If the people closest to him thought he was over it, was that somehow dishonoring those soldiers who hadn't made it home?

He shook off the surprise and grabbed his gear. Declining a case was always an option. He'd wait for the details before he replied. Could be it was something simple like being extra eyes or boots for a client. Hustling to the showers, he waited for more case details to come through.

Instead, his next text was a request to report to Swann's office.

Fifteen minutes later, he was cleaned up, dressed in a black T-shirt with the agency logo on the sleeve, jeans and clean running shoes. His short hair was still damp, but it would dry within the hour.

Swann looked up as Jake raised his hand to knock on the open door. The attorney waved him in. "Thanks for coming so quickly. I've got something unusual for you, if you're up for a new challenge."

"Always."

If he needed to focus on a client right now, he could do it, anniversary of the worst day of his life or not. Thankfully, Swann didn't reveal any doubts in Jake's claim. He'd never been one to wallow in self-pity, but it had been a shock to discover survivor's guilt had such a strong grip. He could shake it off. Especially if the agency needed him on a case.

"We received a call from the Brotherhood

Protectors up in Montana. Hank Patterson has asked for an assist of a somewhat undercover variety. You up for that?"

"Sure," Jake replied, though he had no idea what that meant. "Where and when?"

"Oceanside, California," Swann said. "Just as soon as you can get there."

Gorgeous area, big military presence. Swann had plucked him out of that same area when he'd rescued him from his personal war on crime. Jake wouldn't have to change anything about his look or demeanor to fit in as a local. Although he kept a kit here at the office ready to go at a moment's notice, with the climate differences he'd prefer to change out a few items if there was time.

"Who's in danger?" And would he need to avoid people who might recognize him again?

"The sister of one of Hank's men." Swann slid a folder across the desk. "Connor Brady will be your research and tech guy, if you agree to take this one. He's already started on the intel. Home address, work address, phone numbers and what we know of her routine are there."

Her. Jake didn't open the file yet. "Why is the brother worried?" More importantly, why didn't she want her brother or his team involved?

"She was visiting him recently and apparently took a string of calls and text messages that seemed to bug her. Her brother's best guess is harassment from one of her coworkers."

Swann didn't have to spell out the worst-case scenario. They both knew harassment could escalate to stalker, which could go all kinds of bad in a hurry. He tapped his fingers on the closed file. "And the brother isn't charging in because?"

"The sister asked him not to interfere."

Jake snorted. Opening the file, he read the single page of notes and then flipped to the recent photo, startled by a blast of recognition. Sloan Mathison. *She* was not the name or face he'd expected.

"Undercover?" That would be tricky. Jake had gone to high school with her brother Seth and they'd been good friends. Their military careers had put some distance in the friendship, but they sort of stayed in touch. Sloan had been two or three years behind them. Jake remembered her as a smart kid. Petite build, red hair, button nose, freckles. Spent every spare minute on the beach. After graduating and joining the Army, he never thought he'd see her again. Last he'd heard, she'd been engaged.

In the recent photo, Sloan's familiar moss-green eyes, tipped up at the corners, sparkled with amusement over something. The freckles dusting her cheeks seemed less pronounced, the nose cute as ever over full, rosy lips.

Wow. A dozen years or so had been good to her. The whole package hit him like a body blow. He flipped back to the print out, confirmed her status as single. Interesting.

"That's right," Swann said. "The primary goal is ensuring her safety without impeding her belief that she can take care of herself."

"So stealth mode." Maybe he could get in and out of this case without being noticed.

"Feel free to get close if you think that's best."

No. He nearly uttered the immediate denial aloud. Close was *not* best in this situation. At least, not without full disclosure. How much did his boss already know about his loose ties to the Mathison family? Jake wasn't sure how to muddle through this.

"Any indication of imminent danger?" he asked.

"Her brother was a SEAL, joined Hank's team about a month ago. Hank seems to think his instincts are pinging over more than the basic little-sister factor."

"Got it." He respected intuition. It had saved him more than once down range. He also suspected that Seth's instincts were still in perfect working order. "Do we know if Sloan has any concerning or quirky habits?"

"If we find any before you do, Brady will call."

"Okay." Jake straightened his shoulders and decided he'd better level with his boss. He took a big breath. "I can go undercover, but not in the normal definition."

Swann leaned back in his big leather chair, his fingers tightening on the armrests. "I'm listening."

"I went to school with Seth Mathison. Sloan probably remembers me."

"Probably?" Swann sat forward.

"We weren't close," he explained. "I haven't seen her since I graduated high school, but I remember her."

Swann glanced at the file folder and lifted his eyebrows. "Not surprised. Should I reassign this?"

He didn't want to turn down the case. He cared about the family, respected them. "I'd like to think her brother would be happy to have me watching out for her. A familiar face could be comforting."

"Or she'll resist your presence the way she resisted her brother's offer to help."

"That's possible," Jake allowed. "Or, maybe having me hanging around will be enough of a deterrent for whoever Seth is worried about."

Swann sat forward again. "You plan to just tell her why you're back in the neighborhood?"

"Maybe not full disclosure about being her official protector, but reconnecting with an old family friend should make it easy to get a read on the situation."

"It's worth a shot. One of our best protectors works in the area, his wife is due any day. I'll make sure you have his number too if you need boots-on-the-ground back up."

Jake acknowledged that with a short nod. "Thanks. When do I leave?"

"The plane will be waiting for you at Midway."

"Great." Jake picked up the file and tapped it against his palm. "I'll get out to the airport as soon as possible. Is there a hard deadline?"

"No. Take as long as you need to assess the situation," Swann replied. "You update me, I'll update Hank. Any questions?"

"Not at the moment." Jake paused at the door. "I'll be in touch."

"Good luck," Swann said. "Stay focused."

Jake nearly laughed at the reminder to avoid

any latent vigilante tendencies. Walking out, he discovered he felt almost normal. That was pretty damn miraculous for this particular day and he was once again grateful for the second chance the Guardian Agency had given him.

CHAPTER 3

JAKE COULD GET USED to the perks of flying privately. No need to wait for a plane to clear out, he just grabbed his bag and walked down the steps. No lines for a rental car, Swann had that waiting for him as well.

So far, the biggest challenge was getting an overview of the town and situation without bumping into Sloan or anyone else who might recognize him too soon. He had his story ready and had practiced until he could recite it with ease, with the fewest possible words. If anyone asked, they'd hear that he was in town on an extended consulting gig.

The notifications on his phone would certainly back up that story. Connor Brady had been sending him emails every couple of hours as he continued to dive deep into Sloan's life. Armed with intel, Jake started circling the perimeter of her life within the first days of his arrival. He didn't get in her way, but he went to the beach around the same time she did to surf, he joined her gym, and he found a coffee shop across the street from the building where she worked.

If she'd noticed his presence, she hadn't recognized him yet and that was fine. Even better news was that neither he nor Brady had found any immediate reason for concern. No one had given her any trouble in person or by electronic means since Jake had arrived.

Day three of surveillance seemed to be a repeat of day one. Sloan had gone surfing before work, spent a few hours in the office with patients and now she was back at her gym for a mid-day yoga class. Still a petite firestorm, the woman was always in motion. Unless he counted the serene minutes she spent in the ocean, waiting for the right wave.

While Sloan was in her class, Jake worked through an arm sequence in the free-weight area where he could keep an eye on her. Based on his observations and the information Brady provided, the gym would be the best place to orchestrate a chance encounter.

Jake and his research assistant agreed that it was strange that the problematic harassment that had plagued her during her vacation seemed to have stopped now that she was home. On the surface that could be construed as good news, but neither of them was ready to call this case closed.

Jake changed up his weights and moved to an open incline bench, ever vigilant of the people around him. He hadn't been here long enough to determine the regular faces yet, but everyone in sight seemed to be minding their own business. Currently.

He liked the Mathison family and, for their sake, he wanted this whole thing to be a simple matter of a persistent guy. Even back in school, Sloan had moved through her world with a bright confidence that drew people close. Smart, friendly, and gorgeous, it would be hard to fault a guy for not wanting to give up.

Between the Army and his new career, Jake had a tendency to look at the world through dark glasses. He couldn't help wondering if the trouble-maker that worried Seth had gone radio silent in order to plan a more direct approach.

Time would tell.

He took a break from the weights for a few quick laps on the outdoor track. As much as he enjoyed Chicago, these early fall days on the coast were hard to beat. This case was starting to feel more like a vacation than work. Keeping an eye on the time, he went back inside as the yoga class ended.

Through the glass, he saw Sloan smiling as she pulled on a jacket to keep her muscles warm. She chatted with two other participants while they rolled up their mats. He turned toward the mirrored wall and watched her progress through the reflection. Suddenly, her smile evaporated and her coppery eyebrows snapped together. Clearly displeased, her attention was fixed on a point near the hallway that led to the locker rooms.

Jake blotted the sweat from his face and tossed the towel over his shoulder, striding purposefully in that same direction. And not a moment too soon.

He found Sloan with her back to the wall, crowded by a tall man Jake hadn't seen during the past few days or in Brady's background search. The guy wore a dark blue polo shirt tucked into khaki pants. The deck shoes completed the relaxed professional look. Despite his trim appearance, Jake didn't peg Mr. Intimidating as a member of the gym.

As Jake closed in on them, he saw Sloan's jaw was set, but the flicker of fear in her eyes lit a fire under his temper. "You know this guy, sweetheart?" Jake asked as if he had the right to interrupt their conversation.

The man shot him a dark look. "Get lost," he snapped.

Jake held his ground, his eyes locked onto the stranger.

Sloan used the distraction to ease away and to Jake's shock, she pressed herself close to his side rather than take the easy escape to the women's locker room. A bright smile bloomed on her face and she slid her arm around his waist, pressing to her toes to kiss him. "How was your workout?"

It was as sweet and simple as a kiss could get. And it nearly put him in a tailspin.

"Who is this?" Mr. Intimidating demanded.

He hoped she was willing to keep playing along. Jake stuck out his hand. "Jake Welch." Sloan's hand at his waist gripped his shirt a little tighter. "I didn't catch your name."

The man ignored Jake, his gaze intent on Sloan.

"Jake, this is Peter Driscoll," Sloan said smoothly. "We know each other from work."

Since Driscoll didn't seem inclined to remember his manners, Jake draped his hand over Sloan's shoulders.

The man's face reddened at the familiarity between them. "Who is *he* to you?" Driscoll demanded.

Sloan smiled up at Jake, then let her gaze slide down his torso. The woman knew how to play a role, Jake would give her that. But did she really remember him?

"A friend," she replied. "Well, more than that." She leaned in a little closer, heedless of his sweaty shirt. "We haven't actually made it official," she said, shyly.

Her hand fluttered against his side. Nerves? He smoothed his palm over the sweet curve of her shoulder. "Now works for me." He snapped his fingers to draw Driscoll's attention. "I'm her boyfriend. We're together." He paused, but Driscoll didn't take the hint. "That means *you* can go now."

Her breath caught and she pressed her lips together, letting her hand slip lower toward his hip, underscoring the intimacy he was trying to sell. "Together, officially. That works for me too."

Curling deeper into the shelter of his arm, she rested a hand lightly on his chest.

His pulse kicked like a mule and he struggled to keep his reactions locked down.

"Whatever." Driscoll snorted. "I-I need to speak with Sloan. Privately. It's about work."

It hadn't looked like a professional discussion a minute ago.

"Oh work? Great, let's discuss it as soon as I get back to the office," Sloan said. "I just want to hold on to this mellow vibe for as long as possible."

"Fine," Driscoll agreed, though he was clearly perturbed.

She tipped up her face to Jake. "Do you have time to grab a smoothie with me?"

"I always have time for you."

Driscoll grumbled.

"Pardon me?" Sloan queried, a sugary smile on her lips as she waited for Driscoll's response.

"Nothing." Driscoll shook his head. "Sorry to crash your yoga high."

He didn't sound nearly sorry enough to Jake, but Sloan waved it off.

"No worries."

Jake had seen the all-too-real fear in her gaze

before he'd intervened. He suspected Driscoll had been riding the rush of her discomfort.

Driscoll looked around as if he wasn't sure which way to go. "I'll see you at the office

"Great, thanks." She gave Jake her full attention, effectively dismissing Driscoll.

"Nice meeting you," Jake said over her head.

Driscoll stalked away without any response.

Aiming a laser-hot glare between the man's shoulder blades, Jake watched Driscoll stride through the lobby toward the front doors. He didn't like the man's confidence despite the interruption. "He's gone," he murmured to Sloan.

"Good." She didn't leap away from him. Instead, she hugged him closer. "Sorry to impose," she said against his chest. Her shoulders started trembling.

Driscoll had definitely scared her. "No problem." Should he be worried that she didn't seem to recognize his name or face? There weren't many set protocols for this kind of assignment. And he couldn't think of any rules for a personal reunion as weird as this one. Only one thing was clear, he would not leave her alone until the shock faded and she had that feisty spark back in her eyes.

"Let's walk it off," he suggested, running his hand up and down her spine.

"Give me a minute to change clothes, please?"

"I'll be right here." She dashed off to the women's locker room and he took up his post. He sent a quick text to Brady with Driscoll's name, promising more details as soon as possible. Smart thing to keep it short, since Sloan returned quickly, dressed for work, her smile bright and determined.

"Thanks for waiting," she said, tucking herself up against him again as if they really were a couple.

His arm around her shoulders again, he guided Sloan toward the sleek juice bar that filled one side of the lobby. "What's your pleasure?"

Her green eyes heated and her tongue slipped over her lips. Desire thundered through his system. Had that simple kiss, the necessary close-ness, affected her too? Shouldn't be possible. It sure as hell wasn't practical or even expected.

She studied the menu and he told himself he was relieved that she'd focused on something else. With a smile, she placed her order.

"I'll have the same," he told the young woman behind the counter. Saved him from having to sort out the various healthy options.

"Thanks for playing along." Her gaze drifted to the door.

"He's gone," Jake assured her. With one last, subtle squeeze of her shoulder, he put some distance between them. "Do you need to talk about it?"

"No. He's just persistent." She moved to the end of the counter and hopped up onto a stool. He followed, would have even if she wasn't the focus of his assignment.

Her scent lingered in the air, warm and bright and enticing. Taking one of the complimentary bottles of water, he opened it and drank deeply while they waited for their smoothies. His mind scrambled for a reason to stay close. Not just for the case. Whether or not she remembered him, he would see this through. Driscoll struck him as far more than persistent. How could he make her to see that without scaring her?

"Can't change your stripes, can you?"

He found her staring at him intently. "What do you mean?"

She swiveled around, resting her elbows on the bar, her trim legs crossed at the knee. "Jake Welch, you've never been able to resist a damsel—or anyone else—in distress."

Sloan wasn't the first person to point out that particular character strength. Or was it a flaw? Her expression in that moment, those green eyes wide with fear as Driscoll pushed into her personal space, had triggered all his instincts. Maybe he did have a hero complex. His friend and fellow protector, Anna Lopez, sure accused him of having hero tendencies often enough. He knew how to do the job from a safe and stealthy distance, but after that up close and personal moment with Sloan, he wanted to keep her within the shelter of his arms.

Why had he taken this on? Because it was Sloan. Right. "So you do remember me. I was starting to wonder."

"You're what most women consider *un*forgettable."

Her matter-of-fact tone made him laugh. "Come on. We were kids when I left for the Army."

She shook her head, her lips curving into an irresistible smile. "Unforgettable then. And now."

He bent his head close to hers, his query for her ears only. "Are you flirting with me?"

Her smile kicked up another few degrees. "Would that be a problem?"

"Only if you're doing it to distract me from what just went down with that persistent jerk you apparently work with." The light went out of her gorgeous smile, giving him an answer that felt too close to disappointment. "Is he being persistent about a work issue?" Jake pressed, as the whirr of the juice bar blenders cranked up. "If he is, it's harassment."

She shook her head. "We don't actually work together. Not in the same department anyway. It caught me off guard that he showed up here, that's all."

She'd been downright frightened, but Jake kept the opinion to himself.

"It caught me off guard to see you again, too," she continued. "Though I appreciated your perfect timing. When did you get back into town?"

"A few days ago," he replied. "Not long enough to look up anyone yet."

"Let me thank you again for prioritizing your fitness." Sloan's gaze drifted over his chest and arms. Her lips parted, surely with another question, but the delivery of their smoothies interrupted.

"I'm happy to walk you to your car," he said as they carried their drinks away from the counter.

Her smile brightened. "You've performed enough heroics for me today. I'll be fine now that you've run him off."

But Driscoll had *not* been running. "Something's still bugging you," Jake observed. "Want to talk about it with an old friend? Maybe over dinner?"

Her ponytail swayed as she shook her head. "I'm not as gullible as I used to be, Jake."

The comment stopped him cold. "I never thought that about you."

She shrugged a shoulder. "You were friends with Seth. You both went the military route."

"And?" he prompted when she didn't make her point. "Only one of us made the right choice."

That earned a quick laugh that died too quickly. "I know you keep in touch. He's shared a few pictures over the years." The friendly warmth in her eyes faded. Her gaze dropped to her smoothie. "The military effect is forever."

The disappointment lacing her words leveled him. Something was seriously off. "Time will tell," he said. "Is that such a bad thing?" He was proud of the time he'd given to the Army. The losses would always haunt him, but regretting the effort only dishonored those who'd given everything.

"No, not as a rule," she said. Reaching into her jacket, she pulled out her keys and started for the door.

"Then what's the problem?" he asked, matching his stride to hers.

"Don't play dumb, Jake. It's pretty obvious Seth sent you to keep an eye on me."

"Hang on." He opened the door for her. "That's not true." Close, but not totally accurate. "Why don't I tell you the whole story over dinner?"

The mid-day sunshine glinted off the gold strands in her vibrant, deep red hair. "Are you asking me out on a date?"

"I'm not against that term." He grinned despite her obvious lack of enthusiasm. "You started it." He aimed his thumb at the fitness center. "A few minutes ago you were my affectionate and enamored girlfriend."

She gazed up at the cloudless sky. "You haven't changed."

"Or we could just go out like a couple of old friends who both enjoy food. You might not remember, but I'm a great listener. You can tell me why you're so anti-military these days."

"I'm not anti—" She clamped her mouth shut. Pink flags blazed on her cheeks. "You know that's not it." She stalked out into the parking lot.

At the moment, he wasn't sure he knew anything about Sloan. Something bothered her deeply and his instincts pushed him to get to the heart of it. He caught up with her, keeping an eye on their surroundings. "Sloan, it's me."

"Seth's friend," she accused.

"Yes," he agreed with as much patience as he could muster. "You can trust me to be your friend too."

"I…" She unlocked her car. "I'm sorry. It's not you." She reached out and patted his arm. "Thanks for nudging Peter along."

Her fingertips were light and warm on his skin. A dozen tempting and inappropriate ideas danced through his mind. She was a client. Didn't matter that she didn't know it yet. And although his job was to stick close, to play the friend card as necessary, he wasn't about to abuse the privilege by acting on this startling attraction streaming through his system.

"You're welcome." He looked past her into the car. "Where's your phone?"

"With my purse. I never haul it all inside." She pressed a button and the trunk of her sharp sedan popped open. Twisting around, she set her smoothie in the cupholder and then went around to pull out her purse.

"I'm at the Oceanview Lodge. Will you please

put my number in your phone? Just in case you want to rehash the good ol' days."

"That's all? You're not going to turn all pushy and become my shadow?"

He rolled his eyes. "No." This was all a matter of laying the groundwork, earning her trust so she would eventually open up. At that point, he might confess he'd been tailing her for some time. Thankfully, she didn't protest anymore, simply entered his number before she sank into the driver's seat.

He watched as she drove away, scanning the parking lot for any additional movement. Nothing. The afternoon was as pleasant and clear as ever. Exactly the opposite of his dark and turbulent mood. With any luck the little fake-out they'd pulled off inside would draw Driscoll's attention away from Sloan.

Jake could handle whatever that jerk intended on dishing out. Sloan had likely never been an easy target, but she wasn't alone anymore. Her inner toughness was a direct contrast to the luscious, gently curved body, but his gut said that wouldn't be enough. Driscoll struck him as bad, bad news.

Satisfied she was as safe as possible for the moment, Jake walked to his rental car. He'd backed into a space so he could have a clear view of the gym entrance and be able to respond in a hurry if necessary. Sliding behind the wheel, he called Brady.

"I have a name for you," Jake said. "Peter Driscoll. If he's not behind the harassment, I'll turn in my Guardian Agency credentials."

Silence was the only reply and Jake pulled the phone from his ear to check the connection. The display showed an active call. "Brady?"

"I'm here. Just plugging it in."

With other assistants, Jake could usually hear the soft tapping of fingers on the keyboard. Brady claimed it was something to do with the settings on his headset and his super-quiet keyboard. Either way, the silence was a bit unnerving. Brady had been trained by Claudia, the original Guardian Agency research and support expert. She had a gift for digging up the most esoteric and relevant dirt on a target. She also served as overwatch for protectors in the field and usually managed to keep a running commentary in the process. He liked that chatty camaraderie. Made him feel less alone when he was working an observation detail like this one.

Jake had been paired up with Brady only one

time before and they were still in that getting acquainted phase. Not unlike his current status with Sloan.

"You should be able to pull facial rec from somewhere in the gym." Jake gave a description of Driscoll and the approximate time of the confrontation. "They have cameras all over the place."

"I noticed," Brady said under his breath.

"Nice views?" Jake chuckled.

"No. Well, sure," the younger man admitted. "But those aren't all basic security feeds. A few of those cameras are picking up high-def, full color images and those images are showing up in the advertising."

"Are you implying they're skipping the consent forms?"

"It's probably hidden in the small print of the membership contract."

Jake stifled an oath. He didn't recall any mention of photos in the trial membership agreement. "Do I need to be concerned?"

It wouldn't be great for his career if his face got splashed around on ads. The agency wasn't as strict about anonymity among protectors as they had once been, but it wouldn't be ideal. At least this gym was local rather than a national chain.

"No," Brady replied. "I'll take care of it."

"Thanks." He drummed his fingers lightly on the steering wheel while he waited. According to the schedule Brady had given him for today, Sloan would start with her patients in about twenty minutes.

"Trouble!" Brady's exclamation wasn't loud, but it was definitely urgent. "I've got a monitor dedicated to her building and Driscoll just confronted her near the back door."

Jake muttered an oath. "On my way." He started the engine and peeled out of the parking lot as fast as he dared. The physical therapy office was only a few blocks away. While he navigated traffic, he pressed an earbud into place. He parked out front, dropping his keys in one pocket and the phone in the other. Following the sidewalk, he let Brady guide him to the back of the building.

"What's this guy's issue?" Jake wondered.

"Working on it," Brady said. "Nothing obvious yet."

Motive would have to wait. Jake had enough field experience to learn he wouldn't always understand the why behind an operation or a person's decisions. Frankly, he wouldn't want to be in the heads of some of the people he'd faced during the Army and later as a protector. During his personal justice spree, he'd learned that many times people just made dumb choices.

Was that where Driscoll landed on the scale? If, as she'd said, it wasn't business, then it had to be personal. Maybe the jerk couldn't accept that Sloan wasn't interested. But his behavior in the gym signaled a man who could turn into more than a nuisance.

Jake didn't want to blow his cover or make her mad, but he'd tell her the whole truth in a hurry if that's what it took to keep her safe.

CHAPTER 4

"Peter, let go of me." Sloan struggled against Peter's hold. His fingers dug into the inside of her upper arm. She'd have bruises by morning, if not sooner.

"If you'd just listen, I wouldn't need to be rough with you."

So now his actions were her fault? Her low opinion of him dropped even further on the scale. "I have patients starting in a few minutes." she reminded him. In the past that had been enough to end a conversation when he seemed inclined to talk for hours.

"No one new." He pushed open the back door and hauled her into the sunshine. "Someone else will get them started."

A chill raced over her skin. "How do you know that?" He shouldn't have so much information about how things worked in treatment.

"I pay attention."

It could *not* be that simple. Peter worked in IT. Accessing her schedule had to be a breach of patient privacy or security or *something*. At the very least it was unethical. Too bad there was no one from HR conveniently hanging out in the parking lot to take her report.

He shoved her along, between two rows of cars, toward the retention pond. She recognized his car as the last one in that row, backed in so he could get out quickly. Alarms went off in her mind. She dragged her feet, desperate to escape his grasp. "Peter, you're scaring me."

"Good."

That did it. If the man was going to act like a bully, he'd get the treatment bullies deserved. She dropped her purse, planted her foot and twisted her body into his, breaking his punishing grasp. When he grabbed for her, she lunged into the movement and took control of his hand, using the momentum to apply a submission hold she'd learned from her brother.

Peter sank to his knees, spewing curses over the pain.

"I know you're too polite to be aiming that foul language at me," she said, applying more pressure. "I also know the proper force and angle necessary to push your shoulder out of socket."

"Do that and I'll be a patient."

"Not in my shop." She leaned into the hold until Peter swore again.

"When you're done cussing yourself out, you might try apologizing." She eased up a fraction, felt him catch his breath.

"Sorry. Sorry! I just, you and I need to clear the air."

"I've made myself clear time and again," she reminded him. "If calling me day and night didn't work, man-handling me is definitely not going to change my mind."

"Sorry. Ease up, Sloan. Please. I see that now."

If only. He wouldn't stop. As soon as the pain faded, he'd be back in her face with a new tactic. Maybe her brother was right about her needing protection. At least a buffer. Her mind went immediately to Jake. They'd just reconnected, but he'd gone along with her impromptu boyfriend story as if they'd rehearsed it.

"I'm not going out with you." She would be going to dinner with Jake, assuming he was still interested.

"Because of that other man."

The hair lifted at the nape of her neck. She didn't care for the surliness in Peter's voice. "That's only the most recent reason," she said. "When I let you up, you're getting into your car and driving away. If you try anything else, I will drop you like a rock and call the police."

"No, Sloan. I'd never hurt you. It's not like that. I'm really sorry."

Sorry he'd underestimated her.

For the first time she was glad she'd let him get her alone. Peter's pride was dented enough without adding the humiliation of witnesses to this debacle. She released him, stepping out of his reach, bracing to fight him off again.

But Peter curled in on himself, cradling the arm she'd pushed to the limit as he struggled to haul himself to his feet. He stutter-stepped toward his car, not bothering to look back at her. Keeping her eyes on him, she held her ground until he drove out of sight.

Gathering up her purse, she sent a text to the office that she'd been delayed a few minutes. The second text message was a breezy update to her brother with no mention of trouble.

She took a deep breath and rested in the shade of a tree for a minute. Her hands started to shake as it all came crashing down on her. With trembling fingers, she pulled up her contact list and scrolled to Jake's number.

She needed a minute to get her thoughts together before she made the call.

Not just because his voice gave her a little thrill and the memory of that sweet kiss made her pulse race. He was taller than she remembered, but still lean. In high school, he'd done more running that most of the kids on the cross-country team. He'd smelled so good after a workout intense enough to make his mature muscles pop under his sweat-dampened T-shirt. It baffled her that his hadn't seemed to age, despite the crow's feet framing the sharp assessing glint in his blue eyes. What had he seen during his military days?

Falling into lust with a hunky man who might as well be a stranger was probably a new definition of insanity. Who knew how Jake had changed in the past dozen years or so? Then again, a man she thought she knew well had just proven himself to be a complete and total idiot.

She shook out her arm, irritated all over again for letting Peter touch her at all. Pressing the icon for Jake's number, she waited for the call to go through.

Rattled as she was, it didn't feel like a mistake to put her trust in Jake. She didn't have a better option right now unless she ran away or called Seth for help. Both of those solutions made her cringe and neither of them were viable in the long term. She loved the life she'd built for herself and she wasn't about to let a pushy jerk like Peter Driscoll drive her away from her home and career.

JAKE SCOOTED BACK behind the shelter of the building as Driscoll drove away from the parking lot in a rush. Angry as he was, he quickly discarded the notion of following. No sense piling on. Not yet anyway. If the man had any common sense, he'd realize his error, keep his distance, and eventually apologize to Sloan. Jake wasn't exactly holding his breath. They'd know soon enough how Driscoll would respond to the pain Sloan had just dished out.

Although he was grateful she could take care of

herself in a crisis, Sloan needed some backup. She had excellent moves, but no one should face this kind of harassment alone.

"You moving in?" Brady asked.

"Sloan handled it."

"She did?"

"You didn't see that go down?" Jake couldn't believe it. Usually, the Guardian Agency research and tech assistants were as good as, if not better than, the overwatch on military ops.

"The camera in that corner of the lot is offline. Next nearest option is blocked by the trees."

"Driscoll knew that," Jake murmured darkly. "Had to." He was about to say more, but his cell phone vibrated with another incoming call.

"Jake Welch," he answered.

"H-Hi, Jake. It's Sloan."

"Hi, yourself." She sounded winded, shaken up, and he wanted nothing more than to cuddle her close. He yanked himself back into the professional zone. "You okay?"

"*Hm*? Yeah, I'm fine."

He resisted the temptation to peek around the corner and verify that breezy statement with his own eyes. "I need to get to my patients, but can you please meet me after work?"

"It would be a pleasure," he replied.

She made a sound that landed somewhere between relief and disbelief.

"Should I make reservations some place or do you want to swing by the hotel?" he offered.

"No." He heard her suck in a breath. Due to pain? He inched closer to the back lot. "Would you mind, *um*, meeting me at the office? I'll text you the address. I should be done by four-thirty."

He didn't like the uncertainty in her voice. She'd always been so decisive, speaking clearly or moving toward a goal with confidence. Whether it was the morning surf or making choices about her future. "I'll be there."

"Great." So much relief in that one syllable. "Thanks."

"Sloan?" He wasn't quite ready to end the call.

"Yes?"

"I'm glad you called," he said. "You made my day."

"I did?"

He smiled at the surprise in her voice. "You did," he confirmed. Hopefully he could give her a distraction from that nasty confrontation. Though she'd been the victor, the situation had obviously upset her. "Have a good afternoon with your patients."

"Yes. I will."

In that response she sounded much stronger, more like herself, and he felt better about ending the call.

"You heard that?" he asked Brady as he jogged back to his car.

"I did," Brady confirmed. "She just entered the building," he added. "Those cameras are online."

"Pretty sure she'll stay close to the office the rest of the day," Jake said. "If she wants me to meet her here, she's being smart. Won't give Driscoll another chance to get her alone."

"I'll get to work finding him," Brady promised.

Back in his car, Jake drove a few blocks to the hotel, more than ready to get cleaned up. Once Brady gave him a location, Jake would put a GPS tag on Driscoll's car. That would give them a head's up on any more trouble.

There had to be a motive behind this guy's sudden burst of aggression. And while he couldn't fault Sloan's instincts for saying no to Driscoll, Jake marveled that there was no sign of her having any kind of a dating life for more than three years.

The only socializing Brady had found was her

surfing routine and frequent meet ups with her girlfriends. On the beach, at a spa, sometimes at a restaurant or home. Always a group, never a solo date. Why not? She was vibrant, in her prime. There should be someone special in her life.

He wanted answers to that question and the others racing around in his head.

When he reached his hotel room, he took a minute to simply watch the ocean through his window. The view was gorgeous, the forecast full of clear days good for surfing. He enjoyed countless things about his new life in Chicago, but this view would always feel like home.

As kids, he and Seth had spent hours out on the beach with friends. In or out of the water there was always a good reason to get out there. So many of his memories of Seth's little sister came from beach outings. It was tempting to reach out to his oldest friend. They hadn't spoken for the better part of a year, but Jake knew the conversation would naturally pick up where they'd left off.

How much did Seth really know about Sloan's personal life right now? He'd called the Guardian Agency because he was concerned for her safety. Based on that, his instincts were sharp as ever. Seth had been protective of his sister when they were kids. Some things never changed. It was hard to imagine that Seth would want to hear about his adult sister's dating life. Or lack thereof. Though Jake was an only child, it wasn't rocket science to understand the deep bond that existed between siblings from healthy families. Seth wanted what was best for Sloan.

Whatever Seth might know about Sloan's current situation, at this point Jake would rather hear it from her. He'd gladly accept any intel Brady found, but that was business. Gaining insight from a researcher was different than taking part in what she might consider gossip. Seth and Sloan had always been close and Jake was wary of making a misstep that would put a wedge between them. If his friend had thought Sloan would welcome his involvement, Jake wouldn't have gotten the call.

Jake rolled his shoulders. All of that felt too heavy and sticky right now. He headed for the shower, his mind on how best to steer the conversation with Sloan this evening. Once he was cleaned up and dressed in a loose cotton button-down shirt and dark jeans, he stood at the counter and ran a comb through his damp hair.

He still had some time before Sloan was done with work and thanks to Brady's regular updates,

Jake knew she was safe. The tech-genius had tapped into the building system to keep tabs on her. At any time, Jake could check his phone and watch her working.

Reaching for his phone, hoping for a location on Driscoll, Brady proved his talent for perfect timing. Messages flowed in, including a link. Jake clicked and studied a series of photos from traffic cameras. His assistant was definitely a genius with a dedication to details.

Jake scrolled back and forth through the series of pictures, growing more and more confused. Driscoll had left the office and meandered randomly through Oceanside for about twenty minutes before getting on Interstate 5, heading south.

It couldn't be this easy. No way would Driscoll just up and leave town. Jake called Brady. "Did you find public records of any kind? Maybe an alias? A rap sheet?"

"Only the basics, no, and no," Brady replied to each query in turn. "You were face to face with the original Peter Driscoll. He hasn't been anyone else from the day he was born in small-town Ohio. Came to California for his first job out of college. He's had three jobs total, always an increase in responsibility and pay. No arrests, no points off his driver's license."

"Then what is it with Sloan that made him snap?" Obviously, she was amazing, but there had to be more to this sudden change in behavior. They needed to find that catalyst to put an end to the trouble. Something must have happened to turn such a non-violent, vanilla-average man into an aggressive jerk willing to drag her to his car.

"I haven't found any explanations on my end."

Then who or what had pushed the man to the boiling point? "No medical issues past or present?"

"If he's getting care for a psychiatric concern, he's not doing it at any hospital within fifty miles."

Jake's jaw clenched. "All right. I'll see what else I can get out of Sloan this evening."

Brady cleared his throat. "I've scoured social media for both of them. Nothing that indicates they were ever together outside of a company gathering. Can't find anything cringe-worthy or any sign that he's fixed on a specific person. No implication that he believes Sloan belongs to him."

Jake's frustration increased. That could mean zilch or it could mean Driscoll was smart enough to not leave an online trail. Jake stared out at the ocean again. "Does the beach where Sloan regularly surfs have security cameras nearby?"

"There are a couple."

"Good. See if his car has shown up there at all when she's out on the water."

"You got it."

"Thanks. In the meantime, I'm going to retrace his route through town and see if anything stands out."

"He didn't stop, just drove," Brady said.

"I noticed." Jake couldn't really articulate what he was looking for or why he felt it was worth the effort. Maybe he just needed to stay in motion while he did some serious thinking over this situation. "I'm not trying to follow him or find him." Not yet anyway. "Don't worry, I'll be at Sloan's office on time."

"If that changes, let me know," Brady said. "I'll let you know when I find his car again. Call if you have any epiphanies."

Jake drove the same general route Driscoll had taken through town and, unfortunately, didn't gain any helpful insight. He returned to Sloan's office fifteen minutes ahead of schedule. Parking out front, he sat in the driver's seat and texted an update to Brady. Not a single ah-ha moment or questionable location. Driscoll hadn't gone by his own home or Sloan's place. He didn't linger near any seedy businesses. No curious stops at retail shops. He'd just been driving around until he hit the highway.

The man was a mystery and Jake didn't like it. Still wracking his brain for the clue he needed, he hoped Brady had better luck with his methods. The only consolation was that following Driscoll's trail helped Jake get thoroughly reacquainted with the area. Jake needed more. For Sloan's sake.

Maybe, like Jake, Driscoll did his best thinking while driving. Jake flexed his hands on the steering wheel. Having anything in common with the guy didn't sit well, though they were obviously different on all the points that mattered. Even when Jake had been lost to grief and taking it out on the local criminals, he'd never intimidated or manhandled an innocent person.

He almost wished Sloan hadn't handled herself so well earlier. It would've given him a chance to use brute strength to get some information out of Driscoll.

Checking the time, he took his phone and headed for the building. With his mind on how to get the full story of the altercation out of Sloan, he gave a start when his cell phone sounded.

Jake paused on the sidewalk to answer Brady's call. "News?"

"Driscoll's car is two blocks away. Parked and empty from the angles I can see."

"How long?"

"Within the last thirty minutes," Brady said, disgruntled. "He's not signed in at the office. All cameras in the back lot are offline. No trouble in the PT office."

Jake was already jogging for the front door. "Follow the outage."

"Already on it."

Ending the call, Jake hurried through the two-story lobby, taking in the two people behind the information desk, dressed in security team blazers. He gave them a smile as he passed by, got polite nods in return. His gaze skimmed over the wide, open staircase that led to a mezzanine overlooking the lobby. No sign of Driscoll up there. Jake kept moving past the elevators and into the hallway that led to the PT office where Sloan worked.

Jake remained hyper-aware of his surroundings, though with every step, anticipation kicked up. He was looking forward to seeing Sloan again and not just because she needed help with Driscoll. When his instincts prickled across the back of his neck as he passed the restrooms, he was ready.

Moving aside, the person who jumped out of the alcove missed the grab. Spinning, he put his back to the wall between the windows and came face to face with Driscoll. Again.

Twice in one day was way too much interaction.

"Problem?" Jake demanded.

"You need to leave," Driscoll said, his face red and his eyes cold.

"Public building." Jake held his ground. "But I'll gladly walk you out."

"Sloan is still with her patients." Driscoll's jaw was rigid. "Those people need her. They are her top priority. You can't bother her or distract her."

"I won't get in her way." Jake eyed the man's posture. He wasn't quite on the attack, but he wasn't cowering either. He still wore the same clothes from earlier. It was tempting to ask where he'd spent the afternoon, just so see how well he lied.

"Aren't you in IT?"

"That's right." Driscoll lifted his chin.

"Gotta be some kind of violation of patient

privacy for you to know her schedule as well as you do."

Driscoll's nostrils flared. "I'm an employee."

A pompous employee. "You're off the clock."

"I have every right to be here," Driscoll pressed. "Leave."

"Sure thing. As soon as I pick up my girlfriend." Jake reached out to slap the other man's shoulder. "Take care of yourself."

Driscoll winced and scooted back, cradling his arm. "Leave her alone." He kept his voice low, but the 'or else' came through loud and clear.

Jake ignored the order. "You okay, man? Maybe someone should take a look at that arm for you."

"Sloan is *not* dating you."

Jake folded his arms. "Could've fooled me."

"You're not her type," Driscoll insisted. He narrowed his gaze. "She is not your girlfriend."

He seemed to be talking more to himself than Jake. The conversation, was becoming increasingly uncomfortable. "Get that shoulder looked at," Jake said. "Never smart to let a small issue become serious."

More than once, he and his teammates had ignored injuries for the sake of completing the mission. They were a unit after all. Back inside the wire, wounds and physical problems were treated so the unit could continue to function at optimum efficiency. Unless the team was literally blown to hell, beyond any ability to recover.

Shaking that off, he sidled closer to the office door, unwilling to turn his back on this guy. Something was off. Something that made Jake wary. Maybe Driscoll had a simple case of infatuation. That still required someone willing to stick by Sloan long enough to make sure Driscoll got over it. Jake wouldn't make assumptions or take any chances with Sloan's safety. Especially not after the man had been so forceful with her. He started to remind Driscoll that a gentleman respected the word 'no' but the guy was scurrying away.

After a quick debate, he stayed put rather than give chase. Everything instinct clamored that Sloan needed him. He sent a text update to Brady, counting on his assistant to keep tabs on the pest.

CHAPTER 5

JAKE DIDN'T PUSH the incident out of his mind, protecting Sloan was his primary focus here, but he was a professional. Revealing his unease would only amp up the drama and no one needed that. Summoning a friendly, relaxed smile, he entered the physical therapy office.

The receptionist behind the counter looked up, giving him a bold once-over behind dark-framed eyeglasses. Danny was the name embroidered on his shirt above the company logo. Sliding the clear panel open, he stood up. "How can I help you?"

"I'm here to meet Sloan Mathison," Jake replied.

Blond eyebrows came together over a Roman nose and his gaze dropped to his desk. "She doesn't have another patient on her schedule this afternoon."

"It's an after-work meeting," Jake clarified.

"Oh." The eyebrows lifted. "It's personal, then." Danny grinned, shamelessly studying Jake. "Your name?"

"Jake Welch." He smothered the urge to laugh at the ongoing perusal. "Should I do a turn or something?"

Danny snorted. "If only. That would get me in *serious* trouble." He glanced down once more, a scowl on his expressive face. "Ah, here we go." Waving a sticky note, he pressed the buzzer so Jake could come through. "We're protective of our people," he said when Jake was inside.

That was fine by Jake. Too bad the threat to Sloan was an insider. "Any particular reason?"

"More like several general reasons," Danny explained. "Not everyone is thrilled about coming to our establishment. Skilled experts one and all, and yet, on most days every single one of them is grossly underappreciated."

Moderately relieved by that flurry of information, Jake turned toward the gym where Sloan and another therapist supervised the progress and effort of three patients.

Danny lifted his chin toward the open gym. "Make yourself at home. As long as you can stay quiet and out of the way."

"Will do." Jake moved toward an unoccupied area near a narrow work table. A three-tiered acrylic rack was filled with paperwork and brochures covering exercises from specific joint issues to post-op recovery plans to nutrition supplements.

From the other side of the room, Sloan sent him a subtle smile as she coached her patient through correct movements with an arm-cycle. She'd changed clothes since he'd last seen her at the gym, adding a thin, long-sleeved shirt under her top.

He studied her movement, didn't notice any glaring problem. Still, observation was a key part of his job. She was protecting her upper body like someone dealing with soreness after overdoing arm day—but just on one side.

Less than ten minutes later, Sloan and her co-workers had cleared the exercise gym and the office was down to staff only. Seeing the raw weariness in her gaze, Jake offered to help with any end of day tasks.

"That's sweet," she replied. "We've got it down.

This will only take me a minute or two."

Standing by doing nothing wasn't his nature, but he didn't see much out of place. The other therapist and Danny were wiping down equipment with cleaner.

When Sloan finished, she left the gym, heading down a hallway. Jake followed her past the restrooms, keeping her in sight until she stepped into an office. Hovering at the door, he looked around the wide, square space. A long, counter-height work table was set up under a wall of windows, complete with laptops and tall, rolling task chairs. A kitchenette occupied the opposite corner and a round, laminate dining table with four chairs divided the areas. Driscoll was in IT, but this didn't seem like a place where he'd work.

"Which one is Driscoll's?" Jake asked, with a nod toward the laptops.

Sloan reached into a closet and pulled out her purse and a jacket. "Driscoll works upstairs. Fifth floor. This is the regional headquarters, so all of those offices are on five and six."

Jake made a mental note as Sloan said goodbye to her coworkers. She led the way toward the rear parking lot and Jake scooted around to open the door for her.

"Thanks for meeting me here," Sloan said, tipping her head to the afternoon sunlight.

He was struck by the pose and the smooth expanse of her throat. A tempting invitation. He wanted to kiss her. Properly. To learn her taste and what she enjoyed. Of course, that was *not* on the agenda.

"It's a pleasure," he managed. *Get it together.* Time with any of the Mathison's had always been pleasant. The more moments he had with Sloan, however, the more stirred up he was with a different sort of need.

She was his friend's little sister. There were rules about this kind of thing.

"Did Driscoll give you more trouble this afternoon?" He wasn't supposed to know as much as he did and he wanted her to feel good about opening up to him.

"Yes," she replied. "And, yes, that is the primary reason I called. I hope you don't feel totally used."

"Guess that depends on what you say next," he teased.

She gasped, stopping short near her car. "What a *jerk*!"

Confident she wasn't talking to him, he followed her furious stare to the flat tire. "Let me take a look." He moved in front of her, and knelt down. The air valve stem had been damaged. She hadn't managed that in the course of regular driving. Besides, she hadn't driven anywhere since returning to work a few hours ago. He discreetly took a picture with his cell phone and sent it to Brady.

Standing, he rested a hand on her shoulder to draw her attention. She gave a start, then tried to laugh it off.

"Looking for the jerk?" he asked quietly. "Think you know who did this?"

She pressed her lips together as emotions rolled through her gaze. Anger. Sadness. Fear. He hated the fear. Never wanted to see her beautiful eyes shadowed by that again.

"It has to be Peter. But I don't have any proof." Digging into her purse, she pulled out sunglasses.

No, there wouldn't be any proof with the cameras offline. "What are you thinking?"

"Too much." She swiped a single tear from her cheek. "I don't want to talk about it out here."

Jake reeled in his simmering frustration. She didn't need to worry that he'd go off half-cocked. He and Brady needed to find this guy. Fast. "We'll get out of here in just a second. Do you see

Driscoll's car?" The flat tire and lack of security cameras would've given him another chance to get his hands on Sloan.

Sloan's head was on a swivel as she continued to monitor the parking lot, her body quivering under the tension. Her thumb tapped a rapid-fire beat against her other hand.

"Easy." He moved closer and kissed her cheek, just in case Driscoll was watching. "I know a guy who can take care of this for you."

"You know a guy?" She stared up at him, her soft green eyes going wide. "But you haven't lived here for years."

"I know you. And Seth, your parents," he pointed out patiently.

"That's different."

"Sloan." He brushed back a lock of hair the breeze had carried across her face. Smoothed his thumb over the silky-soft skin of her cheek. "Let's go. Wherever you want." He needed to get her out of here. "We'll take my car while my guy handles the tire trouble. We'll pick it up later."

Her fingers closed around his wrist and she held on. Just for a moment. "Okay." She released him. "I'll pay you back."

"Sure." He wasn't going to argue with her over

money. Nudging her along, one arm protectively around her, he called Brady and rattled off instructions.

"Where should I have it dropped off?" Brady asked.

"We'll pick it up." No way did he want the car delivered to her house or back here, where it would be easy pickings for Driscoll. He didn't intend to be predictable about anything from this point forward.

"Consider it done," Brady said.

"Thanks, man." Jake ended the call and slid the phone into his pocket once more. At his car, he guided Sloan to the passenger side and opened the door for her. He could feel the weight of the day's events dragging her down. He wanted to cuddle her close until she believed that things would get back to normal. He checked the urge. Making the wrong move would only add to her lousy day and he didn't want to be lumped in with Driscoll.

"The tire situation is under control," he said. "Where to next?"

Her mouth twisted to one side. "There's a tequila and taco bar nearby. They have an ocean-view dining porch if you're up for it."

For her—protection detail assignment or not—

he was gladly up for anything. He managed to keep that blatant admission to himself. "I'm in."

He followed her directions and they reached the restaurant within a few minutes. The beachside location was bustling with activity as the happy-hour crowd flowed in. Seating was already at a premium and they passed several reserved tables as the hostess led them to a high-top for two at the far end of the upper patio.

"Service will be slow up here," the hostess warned as she handed over menus.

"No worries," Sloan said. "Thanks, Leah."

"You know her?" Jake queried.

Sloan nodded. "She was a patient some time ago."

"Looks like you did your job." he observed.

Sloan diverted the praise. "More like she did the right homework."

He studied her. "You knew we'd get seated up and out of the way."

"They know I like this spot, so yes, there was a high likelihood." She'd removed her sunglasses and her smile almost reached her eyes.

He could wring Driscoll's neck for stealing her spark, even temporarily. At the first opportunity, he'd make sure Driscoll regretted his bad behavior.

"How long until you tell me why you wanted the bird's eye view and the big buffer between us and the front door?"

Their waiter arrived with two glasses of water, aiming a charming smile at Sloan. "How is my favorite modern torture girl?"

"Woman." She pinned him with a stern glance. Then she and the waiter laughed at their inside joke.

Jake remembered her wicked sense of humor. As a little sister, she'd had a knack for getting under Seth's skin, but many times, Jake had struggled not to laugh along with the pranks and teasing. Nice to see that trait had only grown better with time.

"Who's this?" he asked.

"Nigel, this is Jake," Sloan said. "Jake, Nigel."

"A pleasure." Nigel's gaze turned into a whole assessment. "This lovely woman deserves the absolute best."

"I agree," Jake replied. "Nice to meet you, too."

"Stop," she scolded. Rosy color flooded her cheeks.

"Giving my best is what I do."

Nigel beamed and nudged her shoulder. "I like him. First round is on the house as our appreciation for this lovely woman is never-ending. What'll it be?"

Jake asked for cola since he was driving. Sloan requested the margarita on special.

When they were alone again, Jake merely raised an eyebrow. "Starting to see why you like this place."

"They're good people and the food is incredible."

"Good people who adore you," he observed.

"Maybe."

"Should I assume they also won't let Driscoll get near you?"

Her gaze dropped to the table. "That too."

"How long has he been harassing you?" And why had she waited to do something about it? He opened his mouth and slammed it shut again. Lecturing her wasn't going to help her open up.

"It didn't start as harassment," she began. "He's a shy and quiet man. As coworkers, we attended the usual company social events. I would chat with him, help him connect. When he asked me out, it surprised me. In my mind we were just friends. Instead of turning him down, I tried to explain why I don't date."

"Why you don't date coworkers."

She cleared her throat. "Anyone."

Their drinks were delivered, along with a basket of chips and a shallow bowl of salsa. So far, they'd ignored their menus, so Nigel breezed away on a promise to return.

Jake gave her time for a couple fortifying sips of her margarita. "You were saying?"

"I thought that was the end of it. He seemed fine with being work friends."

Not exactly the explanation he was after. *Why didn't she date?*

"But Peter's definition of friend is, apparently, far more involved than mine." She sipped again. Then lifted her face to the breeze. "Over and over, I convinced myself he was just sweet. A little too dedicated. Walking me to my car after work. Asking about my weekend or the surf conditions. Even when he texted me during my trip to see Seth, I refused to admit he was trouble."

"What changed your mind?"

"The way he looked at you in the gym today really bothered me. It seemed way too over the top. And then…" Her voice trailed off. She squared her shoulders and lifted those gorgeous green eyes to meet his gaze. "He cornered me in the parking lot when I got back to work this afternoon. He, *um*, got aggressive. Physically."

Jake seethed. His jaw clenched as he fought to keep his reaction in check. He'd known about the trouble, obviously, but the slight quiver in her voice as she explained it infuriated him. He should've intervened, to hell with how it would've looked. Should've done anything to spare her this attack on her independence.

He reached over and rested his hand lightly on hers. "You won't be alone again," he vowed.

"Thanks." She sniffed. "I handled it." A ghost of a smile flitted over her mouth, disappeared. "Trust me, he's feeling worse than me this afternoon."

"Good."

"I have no right to ask this—"

"Whatever you need, I'm here."

She stared at him. "You mean that."

"Yes. I do."

Nigel reappeared. As Sloan told him what she wanted, Jake looked over the menu and made a quick decision.

The patio was filling up, but still, in their corner it felt private. Quiet, though the ocean rolled relentlessly into the beach and he could someone downstairs calling for entries for the upcoming trivia game.

Sloan fidgeted in her seat, her fingers toying with the stem of her margarita glass. "The reason I asked you out—to meet me, I mean—is kinda big."

Didn't matter. He'd do anything for Seth, no questions asked. Moreover, he'd do anything for Sloan. She was so brave, with a beautiful soul who clearly left a positive impact on everyone. Nigel was right, she deserved the best. Jake could definitely deliver.

She cleared her throat. "Would you consider posing as my boyfriend while you're in town? I mean, if you're not involved with anyone," she added in a rush. "I know it's a big ask and inappropriate—"

"Absolutely." He took his time loading another chip with a hefty portion of the spicy salsa. "I'm in. And not involved with anyone. I do have one condition."

"Just one?" She held up her hands in surrender. "Name your terms, Jake. I don't want to impose on your schedule or your business here. You're doing me the favor."

Not exactly. He'd only be doing the job he was hired to do. Carefully, so she didn't get mad or spooked, he said, "This is a serious situation. You'll cooperate and trust my decisions without arguing."

She blinked several times and a furrow deepened between her eyebrows. His fingertips tingled with the need to smooth away that spot of tension.

"Isn't that two conditions?" she said, her voice rough with emotion.

"Maybe. Goes hand in hand for me. Protection is my job. This is what I do. Until we pin down Driscoll, I'll be your boyfriend shadow, twenty-four-seven."

She sat back, gaping at him. "No." Her lips parted, closed again. "Jake, you can't put me and my dumb issues over your real job. I won't let you do that."

He shook his head, feigning disappointment. "That's not exactly cooperation," he pointed out. "We'll work on it." He covered her hand once more. The contact was meant to assure her, but the simple touch sent a zip of awareness through him. "This is *not* a dumb issue."

She frowned. "Don't be silly. I can't take up all of your time. I just want..." Her gaze dropped to his mouth.

"Back up? A deterrent? More kisses?" He threw out that last on just to gauge her reaction. She gasped and licked her lips. His body reacted in a rush. Could it be this electric attraction he felt was mutual?

"Yes." She fanned her face.

Just when he thought he'd voiced his thoughts, she continued.

"To all of it, if I'm honest. Posing as my boyfriend probably does mean some public displays of affection. I'd like Peter to get the hint and leave me alone."

Jake was ready to share his opinions on how best to nudge Peter along, but his cell phone hummed against the table. A text message from Brady showed on the screen. Jake read the alert that Driscoll was nearby. He opened the screenshot that showed two dots on a map of the beach, one nearly on top of the other. Trying to be discreet so he didn't upset Sloan, he looked around for the creep and spotted him down on the beach. Staring up at them.

Crap. He could hardly stomp down there and run him off a public beach. Wasn't illegal to stare at a restaurant. Creepy, but not illegal. "He's beyond hints, honey."

Anger flashed in her eyes and she rubbed her arm. "You're right."

"There, *that* is cooperation." He touched her knee with his under the table. "Just one more thing to clear up before we get underway. Officially."

"Funny. I can think of dozens." She propped her chin on her hand and batted her long, golden eyelashes at him as if he held all the answers. "What's the *one thing?*"

"I don't have another client in town. My agency sent me here for one, singular assignment."

The amusement in her gaze evaporated as his words sunk in. "Me?" She muttered an oath. "I'll wring Seth's neck. He did send you. You're with the Brotherhood Protectors." Her voice was low but the accusation was clear. "You lied to me."

"No, I didn't. And I won't ever lie to you. I do work with Seth and I *was* sent here for a security consult."

"Me. I'm the consult," she said through clenched teeth.

"Yes." He caught her hand before she could jerk back, giving her a gentle squeeze. "We're in public. Probably best, especially right now, if we don't have our first fight here."

Her gaze narrowed to a laser-glare. "Especially?"

He lifted her hand, brushing his lips over her

knuckles. "Keep your focus on me," he instructed. She blanched, but didn't move. "Good job. Your pest is on the beach, watching us instead of the waves."

Sloan had the heart of a warrior. From her upbringing or just a natural asset, he didn't know, but in that moment, she earned an award for bravery. He kissed her hand again, held it in both of his for another long moment. "Nicely done," he said releasing her. "Seth's new employer and mine collaborate frequently."

Her green eyes turned stormy. "I knew he wouldn't let it go." Though she kept a soft smile on her face, temper rolled through her voice like thunder.

"If everything had been fine," Jake said, "you and I would've just caught up like the old friends we are."

She lifted her margarita in a toast. "Touché." After taking a long drink, she asked, "How did you spot him down there?"

"It's my job to know where the threats are. And I have an assistant who works remote. Same guy who handled the tire repair for you. His name is Brady." She wrinkled her nose, but didn't run away or yell at him. "Still want me to be your boyfriend?"

She nodded. "Yes, please."

That came out all breathy and he had to lock down his natural response. Along with the pressing desire to kiss her soundly in front of a restaurant staffed with her friends. "Tell me what happened this afternoon. What did you mean by aggressive?" When she scowled, he pressed. "I need the full picture."

She reached for her arm again and stopped. Showing tremendous resolve, she didn't even glance toward the beach. "Peter attacked me on my way back to work this afternoon. He tried to forcibly drag me to his car."

The frustration and misery in her voice, in her eyes, ripped him apart. "Sloan."

"I handled it, like I said. Peter has never even touched me before. The shock of it was worse than what he did."

Again, he cursed himself for not intervening. "How did you get away?"

Her lips twitched. "My self-defense skills are top-notch. Leverage and a cool head go a long way. I managed to get him into a submission hold. He agreed to leave before I dislocated his shoulder."

Jake risked a glance at the beach. "And he's back already."

"Guess so." She rolled her shoulders. "Once he drove away, I called you," she continued. "And I went inside and reported the incident to Human Resources." She reached for her margarita.

"I hope they throw the book at him," Jake grumbled.

"We'll see." She pushed her hair back from her face again. "I was worried you'd feel used by my request."

"Bet you're feeling blindsided now."

"No. Not exactly. Peter blindsided me. What was he thinking?" She shook her head. "You were up front and honest with me right away. I appreciate that."

Almost right away. As soon as he had to be might be the better way to put it. But if she wasn't upset, he wouldn't dwell on that. The problem he had to resolve was Driscoll.

Nigel delivered their food, refilled water glasses, and disappeared again. For several minutes it was nice to just relax over the savory food.

"Did HR make any suggestions?" he finally asked. He was used to working a case on his own, but he wasn't about to ignore any source of help for Sloan's sake.

"Not exactly." She pushed some spicy red rice around her plate. "It's my understanding that they'll meet with him, put him on a program, if necessary, as a condition of his ongoing employment. I can file charges, obviously. They said a restraining order might get tricky since we work in the same building, but it could be enforced."

"And here you are, sure that the best idea is an undercover boyfriend."

"When the boyfriend is you, yes. Oh." She gave a tiny shake of her head. "That sounds so sappy."

"I liked it," he admitted.

She swatted his arm lightly. "You would."

When they finished eating and the food was cleared away, they sat hand in hand watching the sun dip to the horizon painting the sky with reds and golds as twilight fell. He switched it up and got her reminiscing about growing up out here and their antics as kids.

"Is Peter still watching?" she asked as Jake paid their bill.

"Doesn't matter," he replied. "If he makes a move, I'll handle it."

"Okay." Her fingers curled tightly around his as

they crossed the parking lot to his car. "What comes next?" she asked.

He waited to answer until they were on the move. "Probably best if we go straight to the hotel. You can stay over with me tonight."

"But all my things are at my place. Can't we go there?"

"Driscoll knows this town and your habits inside and out. I'll take you back to your condo in plenty of time to get around for work. Earlier if you want to surf."

"That's an early imposition."

"Oh-dark-thirty isn't anything new to me," he reminded her. He'd seen her on the beach as a kid and an adult. Time on the ocean would be rejuvenating for her. "For tonight, the hotel can hook you up with a fresh toothbrush and you can sleep in one of my shirts if that helps."

He glanced over and thought she might be blushing over that suggestion. He hoped so, since his mind was suddenly tormenting him with images of her in his shirt, and nothing else.

"Wow. You've thought of everything."

Yup. Everything that would guarantee him a restless night. "Just part of the job."

"Is this what it'll be like for Seth too?"

Her brother's name was more effective than a bucket of ice water. He pulled his head away from the ridiculous to stay on point. "That depends on the assignments they give him."

She laughed as he turned into the hotel parking area. "You're way more diplomatic than I remember."

He figured there were several people in his life who would disagree with her. "I have my moments."

Parking the car, he came around to open her door. She stepped out, her body lightly brushing his. Her scent wound around him, stirring up more images that weren't within the typical rules of a protection detail.

He slid an arm around her waist and nuzzled her ear. Whether or not Driscoll was watching, he wanted to make a point. "I'll get you through this."

She shivered. Due to the cool evening breeze, the circumstances, or him? He knew which answer he'd prefer to hear, but he didn't dare ask the question.

CHAPTER 6

SLOAN WISHED she could say it was a shock to find herself completely immersed in Jake. Sure, he'd asked—demanded—her cooperation for the duration, but she'd be lying to herself if she blamed her easy agreement with his protective plans on that alone.

It went deeper for her.

Maybe it was a lingering effect from her mild case of hero worship when they were younger. Mild? Ha. Not even. She'd already admitted, to his face, that she found him unforgettable. A simple truth.

As a kid, she'd done everything possible to keep up with her brother and his friends. They were always doing cool stuff before she could master it.

From frisbees to bikes to bodysurfing. When her fascination with Seth's friends took on a different edge, her observations led to her conclusion that the good guys—like Jake—were drawn to smart, independent girls. Most often smart, independent girls with all the right curves.

She had the brains and the curves and the independence. But timing had not been on her side. He'd graduated high school and joined the Army before she ever had a chance with Jake. Maybe now, while he pretended to be her boyfriend, they could find out if there was anything *real* between them. She couldn't contemplate a forever kind of real, but for the first time in ages, she was ready to think about a connection for right now.

Her wide-eyed teen crush on him had sparkled to life the moment she'd seen him again at the gym. She didn't even care that bumping into him hadn't been as random and wonderful as it had seemed in the moment.

Finally in the safety of his hotel suite, she started to relax. Her shoulders were tight from being on the alert, uncertain and jumpy for hours. Even dinner had been a balancing act between Jake-induced excitement and distress with Peter watching them.

True to his word, Jake had requested toiletries from the hotel and given her one of his T-shirts to sleep in. It had been all she could do not to bury her face in the soft fabric that carried his alluring, masculine scent.

She'd been surprised that his agency had sprung for a suite, complete with a pullout sofa, a kitchenette with a real coffee maker, and a spacious bathroom. He said he'd been here for a few days, but the room was clutter-free, the bed neatly made. She suspected that was more about Jake's habits than the housekeeping service.

"This feels like too much," she said, watching him make up the sofa bed. He'd politely declined her offer to help and it bothered her that he was giving up the amazing bed in the other room for her.

"Hardly," he replied.

"Because we're old friends?" Why did it irk her so much to be dumped into that box? The answer was obvious: Jake was a sexy, ripped temptation. She hadn't found a man so appealing since her fiancé had died.

Zachary had been warm and funny, and in prime physical shape. He'd also been a Marine, killed in action when the embassy he was guarding came under attack. Jake had accused her of being anti-military. He hadn't been entirely wrong. She couldn't bring herself to risk dating the strong, heroic, run-headlong-into-danger type again.

And that sucked because honor and integrity topped her list of appealing qualities in a man. Still, once was almost more than her heart could take. She wasn't going down *that* path again.

"You need to be able to unwind without any worries." He spread a blanket over the sheets and fluffed up two pillows. "Now you can." Planting his hands on his hips, he studied her. "Why don't you date?"

Her heart stuttered and her knees gave out. She sank into the chair behind her. "How do you know I don't?"

"Background is the first step in my line of work." His smile was gentle, patient as he crossed the room. "If you were actively dating, you wouldn't need me to step in and pretend. I'm not complaining, just curious."

"Dating or not, Peter could still escalate," she said.

"True." He sat on the coffee table, directly in front of her, elbows braced on his knees. "You're dodging the question."

Definitely trying to. She tapped her thumbs together, going still when she realized he noticed the nervous habit. "Do we have to discuss this now?"

"It would be better, yes." He sat up straight. "Seth told me you were engaged."

"Years ago," she whispered. Hands in her lap, she rubbed the finger where the diamond solitaire ring had once fit so perfectly. "He was a Marine. And a really good guy."

"Those often go together. What was his name?"

"You don't know?"

"I'm sure it's in the file. If Seth mentioned it, I've forgotten. I'd rather hear it from you."

She'd much rather have him pull the information from the file. Cleaner that way. Talking about Zachary never felt good. It left her sore and aching, like digging at a scab that needed more time to heal. "I don't talk about him."

"Maybe you should."

"With you?" That didn't sit right. It felt too much like betrayal. Jake was alive, virile, and capable of protecting her. Zach was gone and all their dreams with him. He'd loved her, deeply, and given her such joy before making the ultimate sacrifice.

"With anyone." The compassion in Jake's voice cracked something open in her heart. "But I'm here. Plenty of time to listen."

"His name was Zachary Bell." There, she'd said his name. One fact at a time, she decided. Hauling in a deep breath, she continued, "He proposed before he deployed. We were engaged about five months. He was killed during an embassy attack. His remains are buried in Arizona, near his family." They'd never had a chance to be a family. She couldn't look at Jake and her skin felt hot and tight, as if she'd been in the sun too long.

"How did you meet?" Jake asked.

"Surfing." The sweet memory rolled through her as if it had just happened. "He was at Camp Pendleton for training and made time to take some lessons." He'd been the hottest guy in a rash guard that week. "One day he asked me out."

"Was he any good?"

Jake wasn't asking the questions she expected. Somehow, that made it easier to cope with.

"No." She laughed, then pressed a hand to her lips, startled by the reaction. Maybe time did make a difference, but until now, she'd never done anything but cry when talking about Zach. "He was terrible at surfing, but he was a really fun date."

"You knew right away he was your Mr. Right."

She looked up into Jake's blue eyes and gave him the truth. "I think so." Pulling a throw pillow into her lap, she hugged it close to her chest. "Yes. I did know. We just…clicked," she added. "I liked his friends. We even had a great weekend with his parents when they came out at the end of his class. They're good people."

"How long has it been?"

"Three years." She ran her thumb over her left ring finger. "I've tried, but I'm not ready. Those first attempts were so uncomfortable. Everyone means well. Maybe he was my one and that's it for me."

"Your heart was crushed."

Her gaze locked with his once more. "Yes." She scooted closer. "How is it you have all this insight? And can you share it with my parents?"

He smiled and something deep inside her loosened. It was like taking her first deep breath after getting caught in a riptide.

"I've been there," he murmured. "Not a fiancé," he said quickly. "Lost three teammates on my final mission. It's not the same—"

"Grief is grief." Sloan wanted to hug him. The throw pillow was safer, if a poor substitute. She imagined touching him would be like putting a lit match to dry kindling. Especially now when she was feeling so vulnerable.

Wanting to touch Jake in *any* way was a strange and awkward miracle. She never anticipated feeling a spark for anyone again. Had seriously convinced herself that her capacity for intimacy of any kind was permanently flatlined. On some level, it made sense that the guy she'd idolized as a teenager was the man capable of revealing that she wasn't as hollow inside as she believed.

"I stalled out." Her voice sounded loud in the quiet room. "Grief sort of froze time for me while everyone else kept moving." She sighed. "My parents understood for about a year. Seth was a little more patient with me. Easier since he was away, I guess. They all wanted me to get back out there. But those first few attempts to date were just..." She hunched her shoulders. "Not quite right. I decided not to fight it. Work and friends are enough."

Jake studied her so long and intently, she was sure he would argue or make a joke about the importance of sex. She didn't expect to hear him agree.

"Smart not to rush it. Take it from a guy who did."

The regret in his eyes along with the hard set of his jaw piqued her curiosity. "You've gotta give me more than that," she said.

"Legally, I'm not sure I can."

She chuckled. "Now I have to know."

He grinned suddenly and the amusement glinting in his gaze sent a fresh awareness coasting over her skin. "It's not what you're thinking."

"You have no idea what I'm thinking."

He pushed his hands through his thick dark hair and stood up. "Coming home, I was a mess." His voice was so serious. He took a couple strides away from her and she wondered if that was it. But he turned, shoving his hands into his pockets. "They did the normal routine. Sent me to shrinks and counseling. Group sessions," he added with a groan. "It wasn't enough. I needed something…more."

His intensity drew her away from her own private hell. She perched on the edge of the chair, the pillow forgotten. For the first time in far too long, she felt more like herself. As if she might be able to *give*, to offer comfort instead of constantly taking.

"Such as?" she prompted.

"No way to fix what I'd lost." His voice was rough with the memories. "Logic didn't matter. I ignored all of the common-sense stuff. So pissed off. More than that." He rested a hand on his tight abs. "This fury burned all the time, demanding action. Eventually, I took it upon myself to right a few wrongs stateside, hoping to balance the injustices I left down range."

"How?"

He winced and scrubbed his jaw. Was he blushing? "The convenience store near the place I was renting got robbed. Then a few other shops too. I tracked down the perps and made sure the cops could find them."

"You were Batman," she declared, totally impressed.

He rolled his eyes. "Maybe. Take away the luxe mansion, cool cave, and secret identity, and yeah. I guess you could say that." He narrowed his eyes. "You don't sound nearly as horrified as you should."

"Because that's too cool." She barely kept

herself from leaping up to give him a high five. "I bet you kicked ass."

"Again, risking legal penalty if you share this conversation, I'll admit that yes, I kicked some ass." Another gusty sigh. "Unlike Batman, I got caught. The Guardian Agency found me. Their lawyers hauled my butt out of the fire, moved me to Chicago, and put me on the straight and narrow."

"Where you now take cases and pretend to be the hunky, impervious boyfriend for damsels in distress. You're a real hero."

"If you say so."

"I do say so." Good grief, he was *definitely* blushing now. She loved it. Batman wasn't nearly so charming, in her opinion. "Remind me to send your agency a thank you note. It's a tremendous comfort that I'm not dealing with this alone. Of course, if you share that with Seth, I'll deny it."

He chuckled. "Send that thank you note to your brother," he suggested. "I'm here because his boss called us to follow up."

"Hank did that?" It shouldn't be a shock. Hank Patterson had demonstrated a deep connection with the people he employed and his care for them was evident in every aspect of his business.

"And you were assigned because you knew me?"

"That was part of it," he said with a nod. "I'm also familiar with the area." He moved toward the kitchenette and pulled down a can of coffee.

Jake was right. She could make good use of the hotel stationery and send a couple of thank you notes. Better than throwing herself at her old friend and new protector. She stood up and stretched her arms over head, leaning a bit from side to side before she dropped her hands.

"Are we going surfing in the morning?" he asked from over his shoulder.

"Do you remember how?" she teased.

"Count on it."

His confidence was as sexy as the grin that accompanied it. Where was the off switch for this unexpected attraction? "I'd like that." She looked around. "But I haven't seen a board around."

"I'll rent one in the morning."

The sensible answer cut through her haze of sensual awareness. Jake Welch was *temporary*. Unforgettable, yes. A nearly irresistible temptation to her newly recovered libido, but that was no excuse to be foolish. He didn't live in Oceanside anymore. He was based in Chicago and she had no desire to leave the coast. Not that he would ever ask. That required commitment and feelings. Not necessarily in that order. She didn't know what he wanted out of life now that he wasn't Batman. It scared her how eager she was to shift all of those buried, pent-up feelings and dreams with Zach to Jake as if she were making a bank transfer.

She didn't want to use Jake that way. He deserved better than that. They were old, almost-friends. Besides, if she crossed that line, it might affect his connection with Seth. Once this was done, she probably wouldn't see him again.

Instead of quashing her runaway desire, that somehow sent her into a higher gear. Dumb, dumb, dumb. She was smarter than this and she had self-control. More than that, she respected Jake and the job he was here to do. There was a better solution than using her brother's pal and the man charged with protecting her to get her over this last hurdle of grief.

But it would be amazing. She'd been cuddled up to his hard body. That sweet touch of his warm, firm lips and his fleeting touches since had all held an unmistakable promise of pleasure.

Surfing with him tomorrow would suffice. *Had to.*

"Hey, Sloan. You okay?"

She jumped, embarrassed that he'd caught her staring. "Just overtired. Zoned out. Sorry." That lame excuse was the best she had to cover her outrageous thoughts. "I really wish Peter hadn't gone off the rails," she added to keep her mind on the pertinent issue.

"How badly did he hurt you this afternoon?"

"Oh." She pressed her bruised arm to her side, as if Jake could see through the fabric of the long-sleeve shirt. "My pride more than anything. He caught me off guard, that's all?"

"You're sore. I've waited all night for you to mention it, but it shows up in the way you move."

Uncertain how to respond to that, she shrugged. "After what I did, I guarantee, he's feeling worse."

"I believe you." Jake winced, then cocked his head. "Was it the left shoulder?"

She nodded.

"Whoops." His lips curled in a smirk that edged toward mean.

She wasn't offended by the expression, more curious about the cause.

"I probably aggravated him when I gave him a dismissive slap on that same side."

"What? When?" And why was he just now mentioning this?

"He tried to run me off when I came to meet you after work. No big deal."

"Seriously?" Peter had no right to interfere in any part of her life. Somehow, knowing he'd faced off with Jake was worse than his direct attack on her. "Did it get physical?" She needed help, yes. Wouldn't change her mind about having a buffer dedicated to preventing more trouble. That didn't mean she wanted Jake in the line of fire if Peter continued to escalate.

"No." Jake snorted. When he faced her, all traces of humor were gone. "No," he repeated, his tone lethal. "And he won't get physical with you again either."

That sounded like a vow if ever she'd heard one. All she could do was stare up at him, wallowing in his confidence.

"Relax, Sloan. I'll keep you safe." His big hands gently cupped her shoulders. "If it had been an isolated incident, I might call it thoughtful. A guy watching out for a woman he's interested in. Show me your arm."

"No. It's fine." A strange sense of fragility rattled through her. Delayed shock, maybe. Or possibly another facet of Jake's effect on her as her body heated under his hands. "No big deal," she said, using his phrase. Jake was so steady, so strong. She didn't want to give him cause to worry more.

"Sloan." She would've found his patience admirable if he'd been aiming it at someone else. "Come on. Show me."

He wouldn't relent. She might as well get this over with. The bruising would probably look worse in the morning anyway.

She stalked off to the bathroom, stripped off her work shirt and the undershirt. The marks on the inside of her upper arm were clearly from hard-grasping fingers. Yeah, Jake wasn't going to like seeing this anymore than she did.

"Am I coming in or are you coming out?" Jake's voice was cool on the other side of the closed door.

"Just a second." She tossed his T-shirt over her head and pulled it down into place. It was huge on her, falling well past her hips. The fabric was thin enough to show her dark blue bra clearly. She could take that off before she fell asleep, but no way was she going without it right now when Jake would be crowding her.

With her shirts folded over her good arm, she

opened the door and tried to breeze by him. No luck. He blocked the door. She gathered herself and smiled. "It's no biggie."

"Let me make that call."

"Really?" She spun around, shot a stern glare at his handsome face. "Physiology and body mechanics are *my* thing. I know soft tissue injuries when I see them. Certainly, when I feel them. He didn't do anything but leave a few bruises. That's. All."

While she ranted, he'd folded his arms over his chest, filling the doorway even more. "Done?"

She nodded once.

With far more tenderness that the situation required, he lifted her arm to get a look at the marks Peter had left on her. Jake's touch sent goose bumps racing down her side, all the way to her toes. The unique scent of him surrounded her inciting another rush of lust. If she leaned in just a little, she'd be able to kiss his neck. Taste his skin. She had to get herself together.

His nostrils flared and he swore softly. "Did you apply ice?"

Of course, here he was being professional and she was desperate to cross that line. Obliterate it. "A couple brief ice massages when no one would notice," she managed. She tried to pull back, but he didn't release her. If he kept this up, she'd need to pack her entire, overheated body in ice.

"You showed this to HR?"

"That was a phone call." At his fierce scowl, she plowed on. "It had to be. I was already running late. Trust me, my patients are dealing with far worse than this."

"We're documenting this." He nudged her back through the doorway. "I'll send the pictures to Brady."

"What will he do?"

Jake cocked his head. "Add it to the file," he said after a minute. "These are deep and I want the documentation ready to go if we need to take further action."

She couldn't imagine further action. Peter would surely get the message after a few days of Jake playing the role of doting boyfriend. "He's making mistakes left and right, but he's not an idiot," she protested. "Peter's very smart."

"Disagree. He's not behaving intelligently at all with you," Jake countered. He turned her this way and that, muttering about the light as he took several pictures with his hand for reference. At last, satisfied, he guided her out of the bathroom and straight to the kitchenette.

She hissed as he wrapped a cold pack around her arm. Grumpy with her achy arm, the frigid ice pack, and the needy heat swirling low in her belly, she complained, "You've overdoing the caring boyfriend thing. No need to go all out like this when we're alone."

"No need? The bastard tried to drag you away," he rasped.

She peered up at him and forgot all about her discomfort. He was staring at her mouth with a hunger she recognized, because she was just as desperate to get a real taste of him. "He didn't. I'm right here."

His breath fanned her cheek, and she shivered. "Maybe we should practice." His palm glided up and down her good arm. "Make sure we look like the real deal."

Yes! He leaned in, hands on either side of her. She found herself surrounded by his heat, the scent of his skin, even the salt air tangled in his hair. Touching his chest, her fingertips tingled at the sheer power in his muscles. "If you're sure you want to," she murmured in a breathy voice that couldn't possibly belong to her.

"I'm all in." His hand cupped her cheek. "Are you scared?"

She gave a tiny shake of her head. Swallowed. "Not exactly." She wasn't scared of *him*, just herself. What if she finally felt all these wonderful sexy things again and then froze when it counted?

His lips dipped closer to hers. "Jake?"

"*Hm?*"

"I'm really attracted to you."

He eased back, his eyebrows flexing into a frown. "That's not a turn off."

She giggled. Felt like a fool. "I just want you to know, *um*, I'm aware this isn't anything."

"Feels like something." He pressed her hand flat to his chest and she felt his heart thundering. "Whatever you're trying to say, just say it."

Words failed her. No reason to talk about it until she actually failed at the follow through. Riding a wave of heady lust, she closed the scant distance and kissed him. Not a sweet peck or a tentative touch. No, she went for it, sealing her mouth to his and boldly stroking her tongue past his lips. Tasting him. Finally. She gasped. He was all heat and pure bliss.

He pulled her body flush to his, one arm banded around her waist. She arched into the hard planes of his torso, her hands threading through his thick hair. He shifted ever so slightly, taking the kiss even deeper.

She moaned.

She'd forgotten the incredible delight of being held, kissed, thoroughly aroused. Pressing closer, she was filled with awe at the feelings coursing through her. She'd thought this part of her life was over. But Jake created wave after wave of pleasure with just his kiss. There was so much to take in, to absorb. She savored every thrilling detail of him from the urgency in his lips to the patience in his touch.

He slipped the ice bag off her arm when she would've slung it out of the way. His fingertips skated up under the shirt, feathering over her ribs, not coming close enough. She wanted those hands on her breasts. On all of her. Wanted her hands on him.

This was madness. Wonderful, sensual madness. And she was into it. Fully, completely. Not freezing up or panicking. The guilt that had swamped her during her attempts to date was miraculously absent.

Reveling in that freedom, she tipped her head back as he trailed hot, wet kisses along her throat, nibbling on her shoulder though his shirt. Her hands cruised over Jake's muscled arms and down his back. She craved more, lusting for every possible thing he was willing to give. Her hands slid over his hips and she felt his cell phone vibrate in his pocket.

He went utterly still.

"Jake?" she whispered. "Don't stop. I want—"

Her plea was cut short by the ear-piercing, mood-crushing screech of the fire alarm.

CHAPTER 7

"Damn it." Ignoring the hellish noise, Jake pulled her close and claimed her mouth in a searing, toe-curling kiss. "Needed that. Don't move."

Holding her against him, he yanked his phone from his back pocket. Brady had sent a text seconds before something or someone had set off the blasted fire alarm. He called his assistant rather than read the message. "Talk to me."

"Get out of there," Brady said. "Take everything and relocate."

"Everything?" Was there time for that?

"You heard me," Brady barked. "This isn't a fire, it's a bomb threat."

Jake's gaze locked with Sloan's. She was star-tled, definitely edging toward scared, but she wasn't panicking. Of course not. In her family, being cool in a crisis was practically a genetic trait. He should release her, but he just couldn't. Not yet. He needed another few seconds to bring his pulse back somewhere near normal. He'd been ready to take her right here on the counter.

So ready.

Her lips were full and her cheeks flushed from their kisses, each breath she took pressed her soft breasts tighter against his chest. His heart pounded in his ears, nearly drowning out the squawking alarm.

"Welch!" Brady shouted in his ear. "Did you hear me?"

"Yes." Jake cleared his throat. "Bomb threat."

Sloan gasped, squirmed out of his embrace. "That's Brady?" she whispered.

He nodded.

"Put it on speaker, please?"

Anything for her. "Can you repeat that for Sloan?"

"Sure," Brady said. "A bomb threat was made against the hotel. The fire alarm is the quickest way to clear the building. I'm eavesdropping on emergency channels and doing what I can to get info on the caller. The clerk at the desk called

911, and said the threat originated from a room that was not booked and should've been empty. Police, fire, and bomb squads are crashing the hotel."

Jake muttered an oath. With a jerk of his chin, he directed Sloan to gather her things. He crouched to retrieve the handgun he'd stashed under the sink in the kitchenette, then moved to grab the knife taped to the back of the table. "We'll be at the car in less than five minutes."

It went without saying that they weren't hanging around outside, easy targets, until the place was cleared. Or blew up. His temper simmered. *This* was supposed to be the safe place where Sloan could rest tonight.

Hell, he'd been eager to find out if he'd made up the sofa bed for no reason. The hot spark between them had been an exciting surprise, especially after what she'd said about not being interested in dating anyone. With her in his arms, he'd pretty much forgotten Driscoll and everything else and he'd bet the same thing had happened to her.

Tonight just kept throwing him curve balls. Good thing he knew how to adapt and adjust. "Have you found any link to Driscoll?" he asked Brady.

Sloan, on her way to the bathroom, jerked around to face him. "Seriously?"

Yes. He shrugged. Passing her, he picked up his suitcase and opened it on the end of the bed.

"I have video of him near the hotel," Brady answered, his voice barely audible above the alarm. "He pretty much followed you from the restaurant."

Jake had been aware. "Wasn't trying to hide."

At least they hadn't led him to Sloan's place. It was a safe assumption that Driscoll knew where she lived, but better to deal with a threat here in a more public place. He didn't want any sort of violation encroaching on her private life.

Sloan stepped out of the bathroom with their toiletries and her discarded shirts in her arms. At his signal, she tucked the items into his suitcase.

"Do you know Driscoll's history?" he asked her.

"No." She shook her head. "He's the IT guy," she said. "That's all I know."

Her eyebrows lifted when she spotted the weapons.

"He wasn't military?" Jake pressed. "Did you notice a fascination with weapons or explosives?"

"Not that he talked about with me."

He strapped the knife to his ankle and covered

it with his jeans. Shrugging in to a shoulder holster, he checked the magazine and slid the pistol into place.

"Are you wearing a jacket?" she asked. "That might make people nervous."

"No," he replied. "People will have to deal."

"Problem?" Brady interjected.

Sloan leaned closer to the phone. "Jake put on his shoulder holster.

"Good," Brady said. "Now get moving. Straight to the car. I've checked the camera and no one has been close."

"And then where?"

"South. I'll send hotel info to your navigation when it's booked."

"You work Driscoll. I'll handle accommodations," Jake said. "We'll talk in an hour."

"Or less," Brady countered before he ended the call.

Sloan shrugged into her jacket, and slipped her purse strap across her body. Picking up the suitcase, Jake hurried to the door only to pause.

"Stick with me." It was getting hard to concentrate with the screaming fire alarm, but he wasn't taking any chances. He put her hand on his waistband. "Hold tight. Do *not* let go, no matter what happens."

"Got it." She squinted against the harsh noise, but her lips settled into a determined line.

He knew her ears and head had to be pounding from the alarms as well. Patting her hand where she clutched his belt, he opened the door.

In the hallway, the emergency lighting had kicked in and a young man in a hotel uniform urged people toward the stairs. Fortunately, no one seemed to be panicking. At the stairwell door, Jake shook his head and kept going around the corner. Too many people were bunched together, trying to join into the flow of guests from the floors above.

He wasn't slogging through that crowd of unknowns.

The next stairwell was further from their car. If Driscoll was behind this—and Jake believed any other conclusion was coincidence—maybe coming out of a different exit would throw him off. He'd take all the breathing space he could get.

As they merged with the flow of guests on the stairs, Jake used the suitcase to give him room to react to any threats from the front. He pulled

Sloan in tight so she had him on one side and the wall on the other.

Thankfully, no one got pushy. Plenty of people were asking questions, others were complaining, and fewer still were visibly upset. Props to the staff for that. Everyone wanted an explanation or some kind of assurance that this was just an inconvenient hassle. But as they spilled out into the night, the emergency vehicles and the tone of the first responders on the scene added a heavy layer of gravity to the situation.

Jake obediently moved away from the hotel, following the directions of officers handling crowd control. When he and Sloan reached the parking lot, Jake was relieved to see his car wasn't blocked in. Yet. He picked up the pace, Sloan hurrying to match his stride. Suddenly, his arm was jerked back and she gave a startled shout.

He dropped the suitcase, had a stronger grip on her wrist before he'd turned completely to assess the trouble. Seeing Driscoll had the back of her jacket in an attempt to pull her away, Jake swore.

This guy was unbelievable. He caught Sloan's gaze. "Down!"

She dropped to her hands and knees, the unexpected move dragging Driscoll forward. Jake threw a punch and Driscoll stumbled backward, arms windmilling. Jake put Sloan behind him, holding one of her hands at the small of his back. "You need to stop this shit, right now."

"Peter," Sloan began.

"No," Jake cut her off, blocked Peter's view of her. "She's with me. Get that through your head."

"She doesn't date *anyone*. Let her go."

"She's *with me*," Jake repeated, his tone lethal. "If you caused this chaos, I suggest you surrender. You will get caught."

Driscoll shook his head. "Not me."

Jake didn't believe him for a second.

"I'd never hurt her." Driscoll tried to look at Sloan. "I wouldn't hurt you!"

"You already did." Jake felt Sloan tuck herself into his back. No more time for this crap. Brady and the authorities would sort out truth from lies. Then they could take action, one step at a time, to keep Driscoll away from her. "Stop this," he ordered. "Go home and get your head on straight before you do something everyone will regret."

"Sloan listen," Driscoll begged. "I'm your friend. You know that."

Jake felt a subtle movement, enough to let him

know she was peeking around his shoulder. "I want to believe you, Peter."

Seeing relief wash over Driscoll's face, Jake quashed it. "Enough." He kept Sloan behind him as he moved toward the car. "We're leaving. If you are really her friend, don't follow us."

Opening the passenger door, he stood guard while Sloan got settled. Driscoll held his ground, waiting for what, Jake had no idea. He tossed the suitcase into the back, and hustled to the driver's side. He started the engine and used voice commands to call Brady as they drove away.

"We're making our exit," he reported. "Driscoll caught up with us in the parking lot. Claims he's not behind the bomb threat."

"Well, that's a load of crap," Brady stated with flat certainty. "He's damn good at putting out cameras at close range. His tech is slick. And new enough that I haven't seen it before. But as you suggested, I've been tracking those outages. Every once in a while, whatever he's using misses."

"Stick with it," Jake said as he slowly left the hotel and emergency lights behind. "I'll let you know where we land tonight."

"Good," Brady said. "One last thing. Ms. Mathison?"

Jake caught the twitch of a small smile on her lips. "Please, call me Sloan."

"Okay. Is your cell phone with you?"

"Yes." She fished it out of her purse.

"We'll lose it," Jake said, anticipating Brady's request before Sloan could argue.

"Good. He's been close enough to you that you should switch to your backup as well."

That didn't make him too happy, but he understood. "Will do." Jake swiftly considered his options. "Can you give an anonymous tip that points to Driscoll? Just to buy me a few minutes?"

"Already done. The police will be pulling him aside any minute now."

"You're good, man," Jake said. "Thanks."

The call ended and Jake had Sloan put her phone next to his in the console. "Isn't it enough to just turn them off?"

"I'd rather be safe than take any more chances with you tonight." Tonight. Tomorrow. Every day to come. He could admit, in the privacy of his own head, that Driscoll creeped him out. The man was way too intent on her. For whatever reason, he refused to accept all the signals to back off.

"What does that mean?" In the glow of a stop light he caught her chewing on her lip.

Danger and threats aside, that's all it took. He was right back to hard and ready, wishing they could go back to those hot as hell kisses before the fire alarm sounded.

Focus, damn it. Life as she knew it was clearly in jeopardy.

"Driscoll is demonstrating some interesting skills in addition to his off-the-charts persistence. Way more than the average IT expert anyway. He's *fixed* on you. He's been physically aggressive with you. Obviously, Brady thinks he's tracking our phones."

"I don't believe this."

"Sloan."

"I believe *you*, Jake." She reached over and laid her hand on his shoulder. "It's the situation that is too surreal."

That mollified him. Somewhat.

"I never led him on," she murmured, almost to herself.

Fury blasted through him. "This is *not* your fault."

She shook her head, stared out the window into the darkness. "Maybe not."

No maybe about it. How could he convince her?

She laced her fingers together. "I never gave him any reason to think I was interested in him. I've gone over every conversation."

He pulled to a stop in front of her condo and cut the engine. Twisting in the seat, he took her hands in his. "If one of your girlfriends was being targeted like this, what would you tell her?"

Her gaze fell to their joined hands, but he caught the twist of her luscious mouth. "First, I'd remind her she was safe with *you*."

Whoa. Direct hit to his heart. Did she have to keep saying things that made it tougher to remember he was professional?

"Second," she continued. "I get your point. I'd never blame a girlfriend for bringing this on herself. But—"

"But *nothing*," he interrupted her. "Stop right there. If you wouldn't blame a friend, don't blame yourself."

"Okay. I'm trying." She squeezed his hands. "This is just so out of character for Peter. Isn't it natural to look for an explanation?"

"You can't force logic with this kind of thing. Not without all the facts. Brady is digging as fast as he can. For as long as you've known Driscoll, this behavior might be off base. In my experience, it's most likely the guy has a few skeletons he's managed to hide."

"Until now." Her voice cracked. "Until me."

"*No.*" Jake smoothed her hair back from her face. "Sloan, look at me." He gently tilted her chin up and held her gaze. "You are *not* responsible for his actions. This is something in *his* head. You might be his current target, but the fixation originates with *him*."

Jake unbuckled his seatbelt, then hers. "Come on. We need to hurry before he's back on our tail."

He kept her hand in his all the way upstairs to her place. Given a choice, he'd never let her go again. Never stop touching her. Protection was one thing. The unexpected surge of possessiveness was a shock. At best, he thought he'd reconnect with his friend's sister. He hadn't counted on all of these feelings. Not like this. He cared for her already. As more than a friend. Way, way more than he'd ever cared for a client.

Inside her place, he instructed her to plug in her phone so Driscoll would believe she was here. "Might as well grab whatever you need for a few days while you have the chance," he suggested. "Three minutes, tops."

"All right."

While she packed a bag, he set his cell phone on power-saver mode and left it on the counter. Then they locked up and left. Not perfect, but it bought them time. Assuming Driscoll hadn't already hacked into the cameras in and around her building.

Back at the car, he did a quick search, not the least bit surprised to find a GPS tag under the rear bumper. That wasn't the standard rental car system. He tossed the device into the bushes as they left her condo behind. Again, it wasn't fool-proof against Driscoll's tech skills, but it improved their odds of evading him for tonight.

"Now what?" she asked as he left her place behind.

He reached over and covered her hand. Couldn't get enough of touching her. "That's up to you."

"It is?"

"Sure." He jerked his chin toward the glove box. When he came to Coast Highway, he turned south, according to Brady's earlier suggestion. "I have an alternate wallet along with my backup cell phone in there. You can book us into somewhere swanky for the night, or we can use cash at a cheap roadside place." He'd rather pamper her, but it should be her choice.

"We'll be together?"

"I'm not letting you out of my sight, if that's what you mean."

She tucked her hair behind her ear. "Yes, that. And…"

He waited, his breath backing up in his lungs, for her to finish the thought.

"Same room," she said.

"Yes," he confirmed, though it hadn't been a question. Same room was not negotiable.

"Maybe, *um*, same bed?" her voice lifted with a hopeful note on that last word.

She was adorable. Clearly, she was either out of practice or had never been very good at asking for what she needed.

"I'd like that very much," he confessed. Reaching for her hand, he brought it to his lips.

"You're not just saying that for show? For our deal?"

"No." The word came out too harsh. She flinched and he immediately caressed her hand, soothing her. The only illusion here was that he was in control around her. He was willing to be as real as she'd let him, to hell with why he'd come out here. This wasn't about an assignment or old friendships any longer.

"If you're sure," she said. "It's wild, Jake. Feeling like this. Still, I don't want to put you on the spot. Like you have to do me some favor or whatever."

"I'm sure." He took a slow, measured breath and forced himself to ask, "What is so wild?"

"This. You." She covered her face with her hands and then dropped them back to her lap with a sexy little groan. "Kissing you is so different. Wonderful. Shocking. I didn't think it would ever be like that again, after..."

He didn't want to hear the rest of that sentence. No man wanted to be compared to a former lover. But she'd been through hell losing her fiancé in action. Jake wasn't a complete ass. If she needed to talk, he could man up and listen.

"Be like what?" It would be nice to have some idea if he was in for a long night of cold showers or something much hotter and sweeter with Sloan.

She squirmed in her seat. "Sexy. Attraction and desire. I'd pretty much concluded that my sex drive died with Zach."

Hardly. He nearly pulled over to the shoulder just to prove how not-dead she was. "Grief takes a toll and it hits everyone differently. You've always been one of the most vibrant people I know."

"Seriously?" She snorted. "That's the nicest thing anyone's said to me. I've felt flat, almost see-through for so long. I know it makes no sense, but when you touched me, something lit up again. Your mouth…"

He waited. She was going to kill him with these unfinished thoughts.

"Your mouth is irresistible," she said in a rush. "I can't stop thinking about the feel of your kisses."

Just wait. He'd show her a lot more than steamy kisses if she let him.

"Decide," he said, doing his best to make it sound like something softer than an order. "Accommodations," he clarified when she gaped at him. "Find us a place to stay."

"Oh, right." She reached into the glove box and pulled out the phone first, plugging it into the car charger. "How far south do you want to go?"

In his opinion they'd gone far enough. He was struggling to focus while visions of kisses—and what kisses might lead to—raced through his head.

"We should stay in the country," he joked.

"Jake," she scolded. "We have to think about tomorrow. I have patients on the schedule."

He understood her commitment and respected that she didn't want to dump extra clients on her colleagues. Still, he couldn't allow her to return to work tomorrow unless Driscoll was in custody. That was an argument he hoped to put off until later.

"Do you have a favorite surfing spot down this way?"

"Oh, sure." She perked up, the screen of the backup phone painting her face with a soft glow. "There. Says we're five minutes away from the hotel."

He glanced down at the navigation app filling the screen. "Great, thanks." Checking his mirrors, he drove on, confident Brady would call if he discovered a tail before Jake did.

"I've spent a couple of surf and spa weekends there with my girlfriends."

He gripped the wheel. "Does Driscoll know about this place?"

She sucked in a sharp breath. "I don't see how. The last time we visited was over six months ago."

"Before he escalated."

"Yes."

Taking the turn off the highway, he bypassed

the place she'd stayed before, choosing the next hotel in the row.

"Seriously?"

"Precautions beat more surprises." Security was his career. Even if the client hadn't been someone with a past personal connection like Sloan, he would've implemented every possible safety measure. With her, he wasn't taking more chances.

They got checked in and he sent a text message update to Brady. The chime of a return message sounded as Jake carried their bags to the elevator.

"What did he say?" Sloan asked.

"Sounds like Driscoll is in the wind," he told her as he scrolled. "Police either didn't find him at the scene or cleared him after a few questions. Maybe they'll get some evidence that puts him in the room where the call originated."

"I hope so," she murmured as the elevator doors parted on their floor.

She led the way down the hall and tapped the card to unlock the door when she reached the room. Inside, he threw the deadbolt and then carried their bags over to the bench at the end of the bed. "Do you want anything?"

Across the room, Sloan licked her lips and

wrapped her arms around herself. "Only you." She took a hesitant step toward him. "If you—"

He had her in her arms before she could finish. "Whatever you need," he vowed. He kissed her, gently at first. Her feverish response amped things up in a heartbeat. He'd never felt this lightning reaction with any other woman. Not that there had been many since he'd been home. His grief had required a different outlet—justice. Although he had dated since his move to Chicago, he hadn't met anyone to get serious about. Easing back, he waited for the haze to clear from her gorgeous green eyes. "Promise me something?"

She nodded.

"Tell me what you like. Tell me about anything that doesn't work for you."

"I-I promise." She pressed close, her lips feathering over the pulse beating hard at the base of his neck. "You'll do the same?"

He traced the shell of her ear, the line of her jaw, to her soft lips. As if anything Sloan did would be a turn off. "Promise."

Sloan would've sworn she heard something crack deep inside her chest. Maybe it was the familiarity of Jake Welch that unlocked her passion. Knowing she was safe with him. That he didn't expect more than she could give. Could simply be the overwhelming, raw sex appeal of his amazing body. Whatever it was, she was thrilled that he'd knocked down the walls she hadn't been able to break through on her own.

She'd missed this. The need and connection of being held by a lover. The sensual heat, the zing of anticipation, the feel of hard, ready muscles under her palms, rubbing against her body. She slipped her hands under his shirt and nearly moaned in delight. "I want you." Wanted to see every inch of him.

He nipped at her earlobe, tugging gently. "So take me."

Lust swirled low in her belly. He smelled absolutely delicious. She pushed his shirt up and he jerked it over his head. There was a moment, her hands going still over his pecs, when guilt flickered through her. But it didn't settle in and take root.

Relieved, astounded, she touched her lips to Jake's chest, right over his heart. This was probably a one-night stand. That was fine. Probably for the best. She didn't want labels or definitions or terms. She wanted to *feel*. Wanted to lose herself. Here, with him.

She suspected being with Jake was the only path that would lead her back to a sense of wholeness again. Daring to peek up at him, she made her first request, "Kiss me."

He obliged, his tongue gliding over hers, stoking the fire that was building inside of her. He boosted her up into his arms and she wrapped her legs around his waist, grinding against the erection straining his fly.

He carried her to the bed and sat down on the edge. Keeping her on his lap, her legs spread wide over his, he whisked away the shirt he'd given her. His eyes blazed with heat and hunger as he stared at her breasts. Trailing his fingers under the straps of her bra, he dipped his head, stopping short of touching her. "I want to taste you." His breath fanned over her skin. "Is that all right?"

She wanted that more than her next breath. Arching toward him, she reached back and unhooked her bra and tossed it aside. He teased the hard peaks of her sensitive nipples with his thumbs, then set his mouth on her. With lips and teeth working, he had her writhing, clutching him closer as she panted his name. She was perched on the edge of an orgasm already. Eager to experience everything he was offering, she reached down to unbutton his jeans.

On a ragged groan, he shifted until she was on the bed staring up at him. "You're stunning." He murmured more endearments against her skin as he bent to kiss and lick a path from her breasts down to her belly. His hands seemed to be everywhere and always just where she needed him.

But there were still too many clothes. She backed him up just a bit. Kicking off her shoes, she did away with the rest of her clothing. At the foot of the bed, he stared hard at her, the hot gleam in his gaze making her feel tremendously desired. Powerful. Finally, when she thought he'd make her beg, he finally stripped.

His naked body was a work of art, the perfection only enhanced by a few scars she could see. She wanted those stories. Later. Right now, her priorities were simple. She needed to feel him deep inside.

She reached for him, but he moved just out of reach. Spreading her thighs wide, he set his mouth to her core. Her hips lifted as he teased her and she gasped as he slipped a finger inside. He knew exactly how to touch and tease her. She came on a shuddering wave of pleasure that rolled on and on. She couldn't catch her breath, her hands gripping the bedding as he continued to lap at her, tongue flickering over her, pushing her right into a second orgasm.

"More?" His lips nibbled a path along her inner thigh.

Her heart pounded in her ears. "Yes." He gave her core a long, slow lick. She squeaked. "No. You, Jake. I need *you*. Inside me."

He lifted away from her, leaving her feeling exposed, but not vulnerable. "Condom," he muttered, grabbing his jeans from the floor.

"It's been three years for me." She peered at him from under her lashes. "I'm clean. And I have an IUD." That had been one of the last decisions she and Zach had made together, but Jake probably already connected those dots. She squeezed her eyes shut tight, and sat up, curling her legs under her. "Sorry. Too much information." She didn't want to blow the mood now, not when they were so close.

"No." He sank down beside her, his big palm stroking her thigh. His blue eyes blazed. "I'm clean too. You want me to skip the condom?"

She gave a jerky nod. "Yes." It was stupid, but she didn't want any barriers. Wanted to be as close to him as she could get. Pressing close, she ran her hands through the golden hair on his chest. "Skip the condom. Please?"

"Sloan." Still, he hesitated.

Rolling to her back, she reached for him. "Get over here, now." *Please, let that be clear enough.*

He came over her, so slowly. As if he thought she'd change her mind. Not a chance. She was too consumed with the needs pounding through her. She needed the freedom and pleasure Jake promised. Dazzled as she was by him, this was so much more than the novelty of renewed sensual awareness. This went deeper. She might not be able to explain it, but she knew only Jake could fulfill her longing.

He kissed her breasts, and then her lips, his cock nudging at her entrance. She angled her hips and he thrust ever-so-slowly, joining with her inch by inch. The wonderful sensation of being stretched and filled, of being caressed, inside and out, left her moaning. He pulled back, then thrust again. Matching his rhythm, she squeezed tightly when he was deep inside.

He swore, nuzzled her neck, then surged up.

Gripping her hips, he quickened the pace, driving hard now. It was pure, blinding bliss. Her body tightened, nearing another orgasm. Reaching between them, he teased her clit and she cried out, her body quaking as the pleasure rocked through her.

A moment later, he found his own release, with a rumbling growl that echoed through her body. He lowered to his elbows, still inside, and claimed her mouth with a scorching kiss. She smoothed her hands along his back, loving the feel of his big body covering hers.

Intimate. Special. Right here, with him, she felt *whole* again. He'd given her a priceless gift, though she suspected he wouldn't appreciate her gratitude right this minute.

Maybe later.

She soaked up the soul-deep, life-affirming moment. No sense denying the impact of what they'd just shared. Her world felt as changed now as the day she'd been told her fiancé had been killed. And though she desperately did *not* want to make either of them uncomfortable, she felt tears burning behind her closed eyelids.

CHAPTER 8

Jake knew about the tears. Couldn't stop thinking about it. In the moment, with his heart still thundering in his chest and her tantalizing scent surrounding him, he'd cuddled her close, hand smoothing over her hair, as if he'd been oblivious. She hadn't sobbed, just shed a few tears before dozing off. He hadn't known what to say then. He sure as hell hadn't mentioned it when she'd woken up and initiated a second round of mind-blowing sex.

He'd spent a good portion of the night wondering if she'd been crying for her ex and what she'd lost. It was a fact that sex could dredge up emotions and memories, good and bad. He didn't harbor any hard feelings over her reaction, but he worried that he should address it.

The morning shower they'd shared hadn't been conducive to a serious talk, either. Especially when she'd knelt down and taken him into her mouth. An experience he wouldn't forget if he lived to be one hundred.

And now, under the warm glow of a new sunrise, he was pretty sure bringing it up would erase that gorgeous smile on her face. He refused to take that chance. They'd rented surfboards and had spent an hour paddling out and riding waves back in. Out here, floating in the ocean, she was the carefree, joyful Sloan he remembered so vividly. She needed this break, the routine that rejuvenated her, after all of the recent trouble.

As more surfers arrived, he and Sloan caught one last wave into the beach. On a laugh, board under her arm, she scampered to the edge of the tide and plopped down in the sand. He scanned the beach, then sank down beside her to watch the others.

"You've still got it," she said, bumping her shoulder to his. "Nicely done."

"Thanks." He laced his fingers through hers. Went with his gut and kissed her. She turned into him, her salty lips going from ocean-cool to white hot in a flash. He eased back before he forgot himself entirely. "We should get back." He didn't like being too far from his cell phone and any intel Brady might have found.

"I kind of wish we could stay all day," she mused.

Her wistfulness struck him. "Me too," he confessed. More than anything, he wanted her happy and relaxed. He brushed a kiss over the tip of her nose. Rolling to his feet, he reached to help her up as well. "Maybe we could plan a long weekend sometime soon." He felt like he was navigating a minefield. "Just the two of us."

"I'd like that," she said, her eyes bright.

"For today, we need to get back to Oceanside. Your car must be ready and I'm hoping Brady will have new information."

They returned their rented boards and walked hand in hand to the car. It felt so good, so damn right, to be with her. He told himself it didn't matter if this closeness was temporary. He would savor every moment.

"Wow," he said, seeing the message alerts on his phone. "Brady's been busy. He says the bomb squad found an improvised explosive device in the hotel, but the detonator wasn't connected properly. It never would've gone off." As Jake continued catching up, the phone rang in his hands. He answered the call, "You're on speaker."

"Fine," Brady confirmed. "You should know the police answered a noise complaint at Sloan's condo around two a.m. I just confirmed it was Driscoll."

Sloan rubbed her forehead and stared at the phone in Jake's hand. "You're kidding."

"I wish," Brady admitted. "They escorted him out of your building with a warning. It took me a few favors, but I finally got confirmation that the police did question him at the hotel evacuation, but they didn't have enough to connect him to the bomb threat. He must've left there and gone searching for you, Sloan."

"Following her cell phone signal." Jake knocked his fist on the steering wheel.

"Looks that way."

"Where is he now?" She wrapped her arms around her midsection and stared out the window as if she expected to see Driscoll walking up to the car. "I-I have patients today."

Brady started to reply, but Jake spoke right over him. It was his job to tell her she wasn't going in.

"Have you found any indication he's done this to anyone else?"

"No. But this can't be his first time. He knows how to cover his digital tracks. Closest I can come to evidence against him is the random traffic cam. I compiled a report of all the times he's been on the beach when Sloan is surfing and it's uploaded for you to use. Nothing aggressive there, but it is a pattern."

Jake turned to Sloan. "Did he ever approach you on the beach?"

"No." She trembled. "I never even saw him."

But he'd been right there while they'd had dinner, primed for a confrontation at the hotel. Anger flared. The next time he saw Driscoll, the man wouldn't get off with a warning.

"Probably when he tagged her car and phone," Brady said. "Aside from that, I've done more research, talked with others here at the office and we took a different approach."

"And?" Jake wasn't in the mood for guessing games.

"Apologies, but I went in and picked apart Sloan's digital history. Someone, presumably Driscoll, has been messing around in your business, Sloan. He's done little things, like tweak the playlist on your music app. Unless you're suddenly into heavy metal."

"No," she whispered.

"He's changed your passwords on a couple of shopping sites. Pesky stuff to prove he can get to you. A few days ago, Sloan, your parents' hotel reservation was adjusted and their credit card declined."

"What?" A horrified expression clouded her face. "They didn't tell me."

"It was resolved easily enough with customer service," Brady said. "Blamed it on a tech glitch, but I'm fairly sure it was Driscoll."

"But why would he do that? My parents don't mean anything to him."

"Power move," Jake replied. "Gives him leverage. He's showing he can reach the people who matter to you." To Brady he asked, "You have this documented?"

"Only that it's happened from IP addresses that are not the norm for Sloan." Brady sighed heavily. "I can't prove it's Driscoll."

Sloan was shaking with temper, fear, or a potent combination. He laid a hand on her jumping knee until she relaxed. "What do you recommend?"

"Get every incident with Driscoll documented with your HR department and the police. Especially yesterday's attack. Tell them about every conversation and text message. If he ever showed up where he wasn't expected, report it. Anything at all that made you feel uncomfortable."

Her knee started bouncing nervously again. "All right."

Jake agreed with all of that. His mind was spinning, considering various ways to draw Driscoll out. "Is her car ready?"

"Yeah. They finished last night. I had them search for and remove the GPS tag. They bagged it for us."

Sloan gasped and Jake swore. "Understood. Any lead on a house that will work for us as a couple?" Preferably somewhere obvious. He wanted to push Driscoll into making a mistake that would land him in jail.

"I think so," Brady said. "Management office opens at nine. I'll get you the address when it's confirmed."

"Thanks, man. We'll be ready when you give us the word."

Ending the call, he dropped the phone into the console between the seats. "Let's go get cleaned up." His stomach growled. "And have breakfast. Could be a long day getting these reports filed."

"And my patients?"

He shook his head. "You can't go in today, Sloan. I'm sorry. When HR hears what you have to say, everyone will understand."

Her head dropped back against the seat. "I hate that you're right." She pushed at her hair. "Okay. But you have to let me speak with HR alone."

He bit back an immediate and unprofessional protest. "No. That's exactly what Driscoll wants. You. Alone. Isolation is a tactic," he said, driving home his point.

"Maybe that's the right tactic. I could meet with him. Come to terms somehow." She shifted in the seat when he started to argue. "Jake, if we keep up this charade that we're together, he'll come after you."

"Works for me."

"Not for me," she argued. "I-I can't have that on my conscience."

For some reason, that response just irritated him more. He buckled up and started the car. When she fastened her seatbelt, he headed for the hotel. "When we made this decision, you promised to cooperate with me. Hasn't even been twenty-four hours. Don't bail on me at the first sign of trouble."

"The first sign!" she sputtered. "Hardly. Peter called in a bomb threat at *your* hotel last night."

After he'd harassed her at the gym, failed to haul her into his car, and watched them have dinner. The man was definitely spinning out of control.

"To separate us." Jake mustered all the patience he had. "We'll stick with our original plan and show him we're together." His tone shut down the discussion. "*We* will file the reports. Build a case. Give him enough rope to hang himself."

Jake would be there to pull that rope tight when the time came. "But I won't give him a chance to hurt you again."

By noon, Sloan was waging a war within herself as she drove her car, following Jake's rental to yet another supposedly safe place. In the last twenty-four hours, her world had hit some frightening new lows, only to bounce back to stunning new highs.

It was bad enough that Peter's persistence had

escalated to physical violence and, apparently bomb threats. Learning he'd been tracking her phone and her car gave her chills. Where would she be right now if Jake hadn't shown up?

She was more than grateful for Jake and, by extension, her brother for insisting on sending someone to watch over her. And that brought her right back around to one of the best new high points in her life.

Despite everything they'd done since leaving the beach this morning, her body still hummed with a shivery, excited awareness. Making love with Jake had created an elemental shift in her body and mind. The tender places only craved more of him. She was a goner, lost in a fantasy of what "could be" with her brother's best friend.

Somehow, in asking for his help, she'd lost control of the entire situation. If she'd ever had any to begin with. Jake and his assistant were not only making recommendations right and left, they were taking precautions while sparing little thought for her opinion on any of it.

Not that she had better suggestions.

The lack of a better plan was the crux of her irritation. She was scared of Peter, enamored with Jake, and couldn't see her way to a sensible resolution for any of it. Her proposal for a fake boyfriend had taken on a life of its own. Especially after the mind-blowing sex.

Could be worse. Her brother could be here instead of Jake. She'd have all the hovering protection but none of the perks of Jake's panty-melting kisses.

And Seth would definitely be posting up, threatening Peter with more than the restraining order she'd just filed.

That had been a real downer. The right thing to do, but horrible all the same. She felt terribly weak letting Peter drive her to such extreme measures. She hated that she wouldn't be there for her patients today. And she dreaded the in-person meeting with Human Resources scheduled for later this afternoon. She and Peter worked in different departments in the same facility, after all. Ideally, they should be able to manage a professional courtesy.

"Tried that," she said aloud, stopping behind Jake at a traffic light.

Peter flat-out refused to listen to common sense or logic. Not when it came to her anyway. His sudden, intense behavioral shift baffled her. She'd never led him on, had always been clear that she wasn't looking for more than workplace friendship.

"Not my fault," she reminded herself for the umpteenth time as the light turned green. Everyone she'd spoken with this morning from Jake to the police officer to the court clerk who'd filed the restraining order had reiterated this wasn't about any missteps she might've made. Some people just fixated on others for reasons that weren't always clear.

Sloan wished for a cut and dried motive over random circumstances. Peter had been a little shy as a new hire, but he'd blended smoothly into the office culture. He demonstrated kindness during the daily routine and had a calming, insightful presence on the job and at social events.

As she followed Jake around a corner, she caught the flash of sunlight off the ocean. Rolling down her window, she could smell the salt air and hear the consistent drum of the waves rolling in. She'd recognized the neighborhood, had surfed this beach frequently, though it wasn't her regular spot. Had Jake chosen the location just for her?

"Wow." Awestruck, she parked on the street in front of the house Brady had booked for them. Another shiver of anticipation rolled through her.

This was where she and Jake would pretend to live together until Peter backed off.

The tidy white stucco bungalow with a red tile roof sat back from the road, leaving room for a square front lawn bisected with a slate walkway from the narrow drive to the arched door. The front windows were accented with flower boxes full of colorful blooms and two whimsical topiaries flanked the front stoop.

Jake stepped out of his car and turned to her, a boyish grin on his handsome face as he pushed his sunglasses to the top of his head. "Brady did good, right?"

"Better than good," she agreed. "This is incredible."

"Location, location, location," he said.

And this was definitely her dream neighborhood. Living here with Jake, even temporarily, would be a taste of heaven. Homes in this area didn't stay on the market long and anything worth looking at had been well beyond her price point when she'd been ready to buy.

"It's a longer drive to work," she noted. Assuming Jake and Brady and HR agreed to let her return to the office.

"Can't be more than two minutes," Jake countered.

"Maybe three," she joked.

"Focus on the shorter commute to morning waves."

He had a point. Being close enough to walk to the ocean with her board was a definite silver lining in her personal storm cloud.

"You want to walk down to the beach first, or check out the house?"

Oh, that was a toss-up. The house was adorable and tempting, but the beach...so close. "Is it ridiculous to say beach?"

"Not at all." He locked his car and slid his key and phone into his pockets. "Let's go breathe for a bit."

How was it that he seemed to understand her so well? They hadn't seen each other in years and before that he was her brother's friend and confidante, not hers. Maybe it was the experience in personal protection that fueled his insight.

He made her feel special, as if every decision was solely based on her situation and needs. She'd felt the same kind of focus from him when they'd devoured each other last night and when they'd gone surfing this morning.

Using the hair band on her wrist, she bundled her hair into a messy bun in anticipation of the breeze near the water. They took the sidewalk past the next block of homes and the strip of businesses on this side of the frontage road. Cutting through a golf cart parking area, they stepped out onto a slice of wide, warm sand.

Walking straight toward the outgoing tide, she paused to take it all in. The ocean was her happy place, with or without a surfboard. Here she could feel small and empowered all at once. The sky was a crystalline blue, several shades lighter than the ocean, not quite as light as Jake's eyes. For several moments, she just breathed deeply, letting the view and the fresh air ease the tension she'd been lugging around for too long.

Peter was a serious problem, but harboring all this fear about what he might try next only hampered her ability to cope.

At her back, Jake was a quiet, comforting presence. "Thank you." When Jake didn't reply, she decided he hadn't heard her over the wind and waves. Probably for the best. She needed to remember she was first and foremost an assignment to him.

The sex sure hadn't felt like an assignment. She

swallowed, determined to keep things in perspective. Their past acquaintance barely qualified as friendship. And they were now locked into faking a relationship as a protection strategy.

She turned her face into the wind, savoring the invigorating sensation. "We should probably head back," she said, louder this time. They could get unpacked and have something to eat before the meeting with HR.

"Had your fill already?" His slow smile set her blood simmering. He reached out and touched her cheek. "I've never known you to cut a beach visit short."

She moved into the gentle caress as if it was a totally normal thing to rest her face against his palm. "The meeting. I'm anxious about it." A lame excuse, but not exactly untrue.

"I know. We'll get there." He shifted, hands drifting to cradle her face. "You won't be alone."

She watched from behind her sunglasses as his mouth lowered to hers. Her pulse scrambled at the first contact, pounded in her ears as the kiss heated. His tongue dipping into her mouth sent a delicious tremor all the way down her spine. She reached out, gripping his shoulders for balance.

His shoulders, solid muscle sculpted by hard

work and a challenging military career, were hot under her hands. The kiss spun on and on and her mind filled with images of those broad shoulders and perfect arms braced over her in bed.

She remembered they were on a public beach when her hands skimmed up and under his shirt. "Oh, wow." Then something else occurred to her and it was all she could do not to jump away. "Is Peter watching?" Had she lost herself in a performance? It had felt so natural, so right, to kiss Jake with abandon.

Jake's eyebrows snapped together over his sunglasses. "That wasn't about Peter." He brushed a wayward strand of hair from her eyes and then draped an arm over her shoulders. "Let's walk."

Right. Walking along the beach was preferable to making a spectacle of herself with a man she could so easily fall for. She slid an arm around his waist, as if they did this every day. Her behavior, her outright lust, wasn't fair to him at all. Worse, it made her feel a little like Peter. What an unbearable situation. She didn't want Jake to feel caught or tangled up, searching for a way to restore healthy boundaries without hurting her feelings.

"I—"

"Do *not* apologize," he snapped.

She felt the tension grip his body. Glancing up, she saw the muscle twitching at his jaw.

"I heard you last night," he said. "You don't need to worry about me pressuring you for, um, *anything* while we're sharing the house."

Wait. "What?" She'd been the one applying pressure last night. Had he missed her screaming his name with every climax? Of course, she'd also been the one crying after that first time.

"You aren't into dating anyone. I heard what you said." That muscle in his jaw jumped again. "I do respect that. I shouldn't have let things get out of hand."

Out of hand? That's how he described their incredible, non-stop sex-a-thon? "You didn't *let* anything happen. I was right there with you every step of the way." And she wanted an encore as soon as possible, please and thank you.

Last night had been like something out of her hottest sex dream. Being near Jake kept her perched on the sharp edge of greedy desire. She hadn't felt anything so intense, so wonderful since before losing Zach.

It irked her that Jake seemed to be taking the blame for something she'd been totally into. Something they'd been in to *together*. "Last night was perfect." She blurted it out before she could change her mind. "I enjoyed every minute." There, now that she'd admitted it, she might feel a smidge less guilty for making Jake the star of all her future sex dreams. "Kinda hoped you'd be up for more."

"Sloan." He stopped short and pushed his sunglasses to the top of his head. "You're killing me."

She stepped back, removing her sunglasses too. He needed to see how serious she was about this. "I know what I said about not dating anyone." Until Jake, she'd been committed to her loner status. "But would it be so bad if real kisses, real *everything*, were part of our fake relationship?"

His strong hands came to rest at her waist and she caught a flicker of amusement in his blue eyes. "Are you kidding? Professionally, the answer is no, we can't."

"What about the old adage that the customer is always right?" She would not give up easily.

"You really want me to call your brother and see how he feels? He and his boss are technically the client of record."

"No!" Her cheeks went hot. The embarrass-ment of that would be unbearable. "Contrary to popular belief, I *am* an adult and I do know my own mind."

"Take it easy." He chuckled and pulled her in for a hug, his hand gliding up into her hair and down to the base of her spine. "I loved last night too. Might've been able to keep it professional, if you'd never kissed me at all."

"You started that." She tapped his chest with her sunglasses.

It surprised her to find such joy in friendly, teasing again. Lost in her grief, she'd pared down her inner circle to family and her closest girl-friends. For the first time in too long, she felt the freedom and confidence that reminded her of who she'd been before. There was a lightness in Jake that illuminated something deep within her heart, reaching a place she thought would remain dark forever.

Trust was part of it, and surely the sliver of a shared past helped that along. But overall, it was simply the man Jake had become: solid, confident, and remarkably unflappable. Not to mention, sexy as hell.

He shook his head, a grin playing at one corner of his mouth. "Not true. You kissed me at the gym."

"Ha. That was just a peck." Though it had made

a big impact on her for all its simplicity. "Here's the real deal."

Going up on tiptoe, she set her mouth to his once more. This kiss, like all the others so far, made her forget the existence of everything but Jake.

"Sloan." His palms moved restlessly up and down her ribcage, not quite brushing her breasts before settling at the curve of her waist. "I'm here to protect you and I will." He took a shaking breath. "This isn't a line I cross on my assignments," he said against her skin.

She believed him. Couldn't fault his integrity. Did that mean he didn't want to cross that line with her again? Selfish as it might be, she didn't want to give up the intimacy they'd found last night. "What do you want, Jake?"

He tipped up her chin. "We will be living together until Driscoll is no longer a threat. Just like last night, whatever happens between us in private is your decision."

That wasn't exactly an answer, though it was noble as hell. He was giving her all of the power, even though she could feel desire radiating off him. His gaze shifted to the open ocean behind her. Did he expect her to wait until her case was closed to explore their undeniable chemistry?

"Jake?" she prompted, when she couldn't stand the suspense any longer. What did he want when they were alone?

He bent his head and nuzzled her neck, his teeth grazing her collar bone. "If you want real kisses, real everything, I'll happily oblige."

Being an obligation didn't fit any of the tempting scenarios flitting through her mind. "Such enthusiasm," she deadpanned. "If you're not into it..."

He drew her up against the solid, muscular planes of his chest and claimed her mouth with another sizzling kiss that obliterated all of her doubts. "I'm into it," his voice was a low growl full of promises. "Into you, Sloan. Whatever you want. Whenever you need it. Just say the word."

Her knees wobbled. Oh, *yes.* She would be saying *all the words* as soon as the HR meeting was over and they were alone.

A FEW DAYS LATER, Jake and Sloan carried their surfboards to the beach to catch the morning waves. They'd found a routine that got them out of the house and gave Driscoll plenty to see if he was watching, though so far Brady couldn't confirm or deny Jake's suspicions on that.

They surfed first thing most days and then came back to the house for a hearty breakfast. He drove her to work, hanging out in the breakroom while she handled her patients. She returned to her yoga classes and he kept watch from the weight room.

They never seemed to run out of things to talk about, from shared memories of growing up, to countless stories about the years they hadn't known each other, to the day-to-day events. In public, they held hands, cozied up, and exchanged some tame kisses.

At night, or pretty much any other time they were safely behind closed doors, they indulged in the best sex of his life. For him, the intimacy went well beyond the amazing physical satisfaction. Having her snuggled up close in bed had resulted in the most restful nights he'd had in years.

As an assignment, he wanted this behind them, but he didn't want to give up Sloan. He'd been hooked on her from that first, sweet kiss and the more time he spent with her, the more he wanted.

"You ready?" she asked as she reached the water's edge.

"Go ahead."

Her eyes went wide, scanning the beach. "Trouble?"

"No." He smiled, hoping to reassure her. "Brady asked me to keep the phone with me." Even if he hadn't made the request, his mind wasn't in it today. "Go have fun, babe."

"Okay." She gave him a kiss and headed out into the water.

Watching her go, Jake did his best to shake off the mounting frustration. He wouldn't wreck this time in the ocean that was sacred to Sloan. Brady's last report confirmed Driscoll had attended all of his meetings with HR and agreed to their demands. He was working from home and taking courses on communication, safe workspaces, and harassment. And he had *not* done anything close to violating the restraining order. Brady had alerts set for any additional online attacks on Sloan, her family, and even Jake, but that wasn't bearing fruit either.

On the surface, that was all good news, but Jake needed action. Answers. He didn't believe the jerk was done with Sloan. Predators like Driscoll knew how to bide their time. Shy or not, Driscoll had invested too much, gone too far, to give up on whatever he'd planned for Sloan.

While Sloan caught a wave and rode it to shore, Jake mulled over ideas from the mundane to the extreme that might draw out Driscoll. Aside from announcing their engagement, he didn't know what else would do it.

And that was too important to fake, especially after she'd lost her first fiancé.

The sun inched higher into the sky and the forecast called for another beautiful day. He loved the glory of the ocean, but it couldn't compare to the joy on Sloan's face as she surfed.

She knelt beside him in the sand. "Any word?"

He shook his head. "Not yet." He wasn't in the water, but just sitting here restored him. The sound of the ocean rushing to shore was a relentless and tranquil reminder of how big and powerful the world was outside of this moment.

They were caught between a crisis point and sweet contentment. When Sloan was near, Jake felt like he could conquer any challenge as long as she was waiting for him on the other side.

He slipped a hand up into her hair and pulled her mouth to his, feathering a kiss over her sweet lips. Thoroughly distracted by her, it took a second for the shouts behind them to register.

"Look out!" Another surfer, ran at them, pointing over Jake's shoulder.

Twisting, he saw a drone coming straight at him. As he rolled to his feet, the device lifted up, pitching erratically until it balanced again. Then it swooped low and came at him again.

"Driscoll." Had to be. He pulled his phone from inside the jacket he'd worn. "Can you spot the operator?" he asked Sloan.

"No one in sight," she replied.

"Keep looking and stay low. Better yet, get back out on the water."

She shook her head. "I'm not leaving you."

He didn't know the ranges on these things, but Brady would. He took a couple of pictures before calling his assistant. "Drones," he barked into the phone. "He's been watching us with drones."

Scanning the area, he started for the nearest life guard tower about a hundred yards away. It wasn't manned at this hour and would be the perfect shelter for someone who wanted to operate a drone without being seen.

"Jake! Look out!"

He heard the buzz at the same time Sloan's warning reached him. He dropped to a crouch a half-second too late. The machine clipped him on the shoulder, knocking him over. He had to roll to recover and by the time he'd righted himself, Sloan was right there.

"I'm good," he promised her. Not a bad hit. "Drone got the worst of it." Scrambling across the sand, he caught the floundering device before it landed in the water.

He pressed his phone into her hands. "Call the cops."

"You're bleeding!"

"No big deal." He dropped the disabled drone beside her as well. "I need to check the tower." Moving that way, he saw a skinny guy scramble over the tower railing and dart up to the road. Too young to be Driscoll, wrong build, but Jake was sure they were connected. He started to give chase, and stopped. No way would he leave Sloan exposed. All he could do was watch as the guy hopped into a car and got away.

By the time the police arrived, he'd given Brady a full report, relaying as much information about the drone and the guy who'd run from the lifeguard tower as he could. Between the local authorities and his assistant, if Driscoll was launching drones or enlisting help to spy on Sloan, the details would come to light soon enough.

"We need to get this cleaned up," Sloan said, eyeing his shoulder with concern. "Can you manage the surfboard?"

Was she serious? "Of course."

"Don't get grumpy with me just because I care."

"Sorry." He kissed her softly. "I'm grumpy that a machine tagged me. Thank you for caring."

With a sigh, her supple body pressed closer.

"I didn't expect this," he murmured against her lips. "Didn't expect you."

Her slender, warm fingers curled around his wrists, resting over his pounding pulse. "Neither did I." She licked her lips. "My unconventional suggestion has turned into something so much more. You're more than a friend or bodyguard. You've gone above and beyond anything an old friend should ask."

"You're more than that to me," he said.

"Same goes." She smiled and he would've sworn he saw the stars twinkling in her eyes.

He kissed her with all of the feelings he should just put into words. She was more than Seth's sister. More than a friend. Sloan had become his world. He'd fallen in love with her. Lips trailing along her jaw, up to her ear, he gently nibbled on her earlobe, down her throat. "I love you, Sloan."

Though he'd whispered it against her skin, he knew she'd heard. Her body went stiff within his embrace. "Oh, Jake."

"Shh." He soothed her with more soft kisses and light touches, feeling her relax by one slow degree after another. "You don't have to do anything. Say anything. No such thing as a required response. Just couldn't keep it locked down anymore." He filled his palms with the sweet curves of her hips, then brought them up, stroking her spine until she arched into him.

Distracting them both from his ill-timed declaration was essential. He didn't want to hear a denial or another explanation of why she refused to have a relationship with a military-type man. His heart was hers, simple fact. He breathed her in, sipped from her lips. His longing for her taste, her laughter, her joyful smile wasn't going to change. She might walk away when his assignment was complete, but whatever came next, part of his heart would always be right here with her.

The pulse at the base of her throat fluttered under his lips and tongue. With the ocean racing up the sand, sliding over their ankles and sucking the sand from under his feet on the return to the sea, he kept kissing and teasing until she murmured nonsense in his ear, against his lips. Only then did it feel safe enough to slow down, put the passion on pause until they returned to the privacy of the rental house.

She was quiet on the walk back, but he knew he wasn't in the clear yet. Not by a long shot. When their boards were stored around back, she caught his hand in both of hers.

"Jake?" He would've happily given her some

breathing room. Time to process his wild declaration. "This means something to me."

His chest was caught in the vise of faint praise. Worse than a sucker-punch, better than a bullet. He breathed through it, but he couldn't quite summon a smile. "I'm glad."

Sloan wasn't the easy, careless type. She never would've made love with him, bared her body and soul, without the connection of real feelings. "Really, there's no pressure," he managed, his breath backed up in his lungs. "As long as you're safe and happy, that's enough for me."

She released him, her hands balling into fists at her sides. "It shouldn't be. You deserve the whole package, Jake. A woman who appreciates you. Someone who can love you."

Was she still in love with her fiancé? It made sense, but damn it hurt.

He told himself to be patient and smothered the urge to argue. Did she think he missed the way she melted when they were in bed? Or the way she confided her fears as well as her hopes for the future? He'd had casual sex. What he felt with Sloan crushed that boundary.

"You're right," he said instead. His heart was convinced that woman was her. "And there's plenty of time for all those forever things, down the road. Right now, I'm enjoying being with you in addition to fulfilling my assignment to protect you. You don't need to worry about hurting my feelings, Sloan."

She cocked her head, narrowed her eyes. "You mean that."

"I do." He winked, then turned to pull open the back door. "We need to get moving or you'll be late to work."

"We have enough time to take care of that wound," she said, lifting her chin. "You hit the shower while I start breakfast. Then I can bandage it for you before I clean up."

The wound wasn't that bad. Amused, he kissed her as she marched into the house ahead of him. Yeah, she was it for him. He could only hope one day she reached the same conclusion.

A WEEK after the drone attack, Sloan and Jake were out on the beach as twilight fell. Neither one of them could seem to get enough of this quiet little pocket of coastline. How much longer would she have these moments with him?

It should've been the perfect autumn evening. The cool breeze lifted her hair, the steady beat of waves rushing into shore, and the man she'd fallen in love with at her side. She really should tell him how she felt. He'd taken a big chance revealing his feelings. She just didn't want him to think she'd confused protection with the real deal, or somehow felt pressured by his feelings for her.

It would be nearly impossible to convince him when she viewed every person out here as a potential threat. No one had seen Peter for several days. The police had questioned the guy who had operated the drone from the lifeguard tower, but it had been an online, no-name transaction.

A dead end.

Although there hadn't been any more direct trouble, she agreed with Jake's assessment that Driscoll wasn't done. With either of them. The digital records showed he was supposedly still working from home while going through the additional training requirements for HR, but she was sure he'd been manipulating the system. Brady had confirmed other drones in the area over the beach and their house, but he had yet to conclusively tie those flights to Peter.

Peter could be anywhere and she *knew* he was

watching her. It was a prickle of uneasy awareness caught between her shoulder blades that would *not* let up.

"I wish I understood why he latched on to me."

"Only a skilled professional will sort that out," Jake said. "And only if Driscoll is willing to change. We have to stay vigilant until he's cleared or does something to land himself in jail."

It was obvious to her which outcome Jake preferred.

"We're in a holding pattern, yes. But he doesn't call the shots, Sloan." He hugged her close. "We can be patient."

She paused as the ocean chased up the beach and lapped at her toes. Curling into his embrace, she wrapped her arms around him. With her cheek against his chest, she breathed him in. Patience wasn't working for her. She loved this time with Jake, but she wanted to be with him and wanted him to be with her because it was an option, not a necessary role they were playing.

"You're thinking about the note," Jake said.

"Yes," she admitted.

Snuggling in, she watched the ocean ebb and flow, but the creepy note they'd found in her locker this morning still haunted her. *"Meet me alone or Welch dies."*

Peter hadn't signed it. Hadn't even written it by hand. One more disconnected threat from a man who had gone off the rails. Not that she had any doubts that he was behind it. Only Peter had reason to make that kind of threat. Building security had no record of him entering the break room. Just one more example of his technical wizardry. Brady had been as livid as Jake.

Sloan was terrified in addition to furious. After lunch, she'd found a second note clipped inside a patient file with an address and time for the meeting. She hadn't shown that to Jake yet. Call her a fool, but she wasn't going to let him walk into a trap. They'd argued about how to proceed after finding the first note, since he didn't want her walking into a trap either.

Peter had stated over and over that he didn't want to hurt her. She was counting on that promise, planning to lean into it so he would see reason. If Jake got hurt trying to protect her, it would be more than she could bear. Life had taken enough from her. She couldn't lose Jake too.

She didn't know what Peter wanted from her. Didn't have any idea how she'd convince him to leave her alone, but she refused to let this game of intimidation continue. Whether or not her relationship with Jake was as real as it felt to her, he couldn't stay in California. His career was based in Chicago. The Guardian Agency couldn't watch over her and the people she loved indefinitely.

"I won't face him without you," she said. Jake needed to hear that, even if it was a fib. She'd take precautions and go to the meeting. They weren't free to talk about a possible future until Peter was out of their lives.

His chest rose and fell on a sigh. Pressing a kiss to the top of her head, he said, "Thank you."

The power to end this was on her shoulders and she wouldn't cower from that responsibility. Her decision made, they finished their beach walk in a sweet, companionable silence and then headed back to the bungalow.

CHAPTER 10

THE HARDEST THING Jake had ever done was remain still and keep his breath steady as Sloan eased away from his embrace and out of the bed. He waited while every instinct he had clamored for him to chase her down. Keep her close. Keep her safe.

He was more grateful than ever that he and Brady had taken precautions. Called in reinforcements for just this scenario.

With nothing better to do for the next minute or so, he stewed in frustration. *She'd lied.* Told him she wouldn't face Driscoll alone.

He wanted to be hurt by that lie. She should trust him by now. But he couldn't really hold it against her. He'd lied as well, implying that he believed her promise, when he'd known all along that she felt responsible and wanted to protect *him*.

That only made him want to rage over the entire situation. Had to give Driscoll credit for finding the right leverage. Too bad Jake hadn't earned Sloan's confidence. The woman could be so stubborn. In most circumstances he considered her tenacity a strength. Not tonight.

Would that be something they could work on when the crisis was over? Or was he hoping for more than she wanted to give? He wanted forever with Sloan. Side by side. As a team. He wanted Sloan to be his partner for life. Although he wasn't sure they were off to the best start, he wouldn't give up on their future just yet.

Hearing her slip out the front door, he rolled over to grab his phone off the nightstand. Called Brady. "She just left," he said when his assistant picked up. "Tell me you're watching her."

"Every move," Brady confirmed.

"Any chance Driscoll can interfere with our comms?" The jerk had proved remarkably resourceful with technology.

"There's a chance," Brady allowed. "It's low enough to not be a factor."

Jake appreciated the confidence and the candor. "What haven't you told me?"

"I know where Driscoll set the meeting. Her brother is on site."

Jake felt a prickle of failure under his skin. He should've figured that out, anticipated how the bastard would reel in Sloan. "Details, Brady. Now."

"Just sent over the address and directions, if necessary."

If necessary? What the hell did that mean? "I'll be on my way in less than five." Even that felt like leaving Sloan exposed for way too long.

"Shut up and get down," Brady snapped. "Action at the window."

Jake obeyed, though it made no sense. The security lights should've come on if someone was out there. Tucked in a low crouch at the side of the bed, he peeked over the rumpled covers in time to see a shadow of movement. "Driscoll?" he asked via text message.

Brady sent confirmation immediately.

Suddenly relieved that Sloan was out of harm's way, Jake tugged on a pair of gym shorts, returned his phone to the nightstand, grabbed his gun, and was ready to rumble.

Paused at the bedroom doorway, he heard the

creak of the flooring just inside the back door. Driscoll was on the offensive. Must've set this up to eliminate Jake. What story would the creep give Sloan as he moved in to comfort her? Jake shook off that unpleasant thought. Sloan would never fall for Driscoll's crap.

Besides, Jake wouldn't let him get the chance. Hearing footsteps in the hallway, Jake held his position behind the bedroom door. The door eased open and the barrel of a shotgun appeared first.

"Jake?"

He flinched.

The shotgun barrel froze.

Suddenly light flooded the hallway from the fixture overhead.

Sloan. This might be the one time in his life when he didn't want to see her. When had she doubled back? Jake was ready to throttle Brady for the lack of warning when he realized he didn't have his phone or an earbud.

Jake jumped up and slammed all of his weight into the door. He caught Driscoll at the shoulder and the gun blasted buckshot into the floor before Jake could wrestle it out of his grasp.

"Peter!" Sloan shouted as the booming sound faded. "What are you doing?"

Jake tossed his gun to the bed and kicked the shotgun out of reach. He would take no chances with Sloan so close. He came around the door and launched himself at Driscoll, driving him to the floor. The man had zero chance. Jake swatted away his weak punches, crushing his ribcage between his knees until he was gasping for air.

"Call the police." Jake grunted as Driscoll squirmed.

"No! Sloan!" Driscoll twisted his head around, trying to see her. "Please. I'm sorry."

To Jake's horror, she stomped closer. "Police, Sloan."

"They're already on the way."

She was too close, nearly within Driscoll's reach. Jake moved quickly, pulling the jerk's arms behind his back. "You do not touch her."

Sloan met his gaze and took a quick step back. Then she pinned Driscoll with a hard glare. "I called the police when I saw your car two blocks over."

Good, good. Brady would react accordingly and their team would be closing in.

"No. You don't understand," Driscoll pleaded. His body went rigid as he tried to buck Jake off. He relented when he made no progress. "Sloan, we belong together, you're supposed to be at *our* place. Not here. *Not here.*"

Our place? Something in the man's voice cut through Jake's temper and details snapped into place. There was a certain sick logic in this attack. He'd bet his life on being right, but not Sloan's. "Get out, Sloan."

Sirens sounded.

"Go meet the police," Jake added more gently. "Go on, sweetheart. Tell them who's who in here."

"But—"

Driscoll bucked again, taking advantage of Jake's distraction to get his arms free. He scrambled on hands and knees, almost catching Sloan. "I'll surrender," he declared. "Walk me out, Sloan. I'll surrender."

Of course, he would. The bastard had turned this place into a trap of some sort. Jake snagged Driscoll's ankle, hauled him back. "We're right behind you." He tried to smile. "Let them know we're unarmed."

Her lips parted again, but whatever she saw in his face, stopped her cold. She turned abruptly and ran for the door. He nearly sagged with relief.

"Where is it?" Jake snarled when she was out of earshot. "I know you planted a bomb. How did you plan to detonate it?" He gave Driscoll a hard shake.

"It's too late." Driscoll smiled. A sloppy, resigned expression. "Too late. If I can't have her, neither will you."

Like hell. He looked around. Thought about everything they'd learned about Driscoll. He wasn't any kind of expert with explosives. Didn't have any kind of military experience. What he did have was the ability to research anything and a penchant for technology.

"Think how much you'll hurt her if we both die here." Jake hauled Driscoll to his feet. "Only a bastard would set her up for that kind of pain." When they started toward the bedroom, Driscoll showed another burst of resistance.

No surprise. In a few deft moves, Jake had full control of Driscoll. He shoved the man ahead of him into the bedroom. "It's too late," Driscoll insisted.

Jake kicked the door shut behind them. Both guns were out of easy reach, but Jake didn't need anything but his hands to end Driscoll. For Sloan, he wanted to do this right. And he sure as hell wanted to live through it.

"Live or die, man. Your call. Tell me where you

planted it." Then he'd face the pertinent issue of whether or not he could disarm the device. The Army had trained him in the basics, but there were too many factors in play for him to be certain about anything.

The bastard was too smug. He had arranged for Sloan to be out of the house, yet he'd come into the bedroom with a shotgun. "I get it," Jake said, thinking aloud. "You shoot me in my sleep, the bomb takes care of any evidence and you have an alibi in Sloan. But you didn't count on Sloan being so observant. Or me being so hard to kill."

On a surge of survival-instinct, Driscoll lurched out of Jake's grasp. He rushed toward the bedroom window, the only other way out. Tripping over the shotgun, he grabbed it and turned, aiming it at Jake. "You're going to stay here while I escape."

Ignoring the idiot, Jake hit the switch for the overhead light and dropped down to inspect the underside of the bed. Sure enough, he saw a pipe bomb, glowing with a simple electronic timer that was counting down. When he got out of here, Jake and Brady were going to figure out how Driscoll had managed to plant the damn thing.

"I'll shoot if you try to follow me."

"Go ahead." On his belly, Jake crawled closer to the center of the bed. "The police outside will love that."

Now he was thankful Sloan had decided to go face Driscoll on her own. If she'd stayed with him tonight, they might've both wound up dead.

He heard a crash as Driscoll broke the window. Then the shotgun blasted again. Buckshot pellets tore through the mattress and frame, narrowly missing the bomb and scoring Jake's flesh in a few places.

He didn't waste time whining about it. His focus was on disconnecting the timer. It wasn't a complex device, but arrogance could be deadly. He heard voices raised outside and grinned despite it all when he heard Seth barking orders.

"Help me!" Driscoll shouted.

Facing the dangerous explosive, Jake pushed aside his curiosity about how the ass would explain the shotgun blast and the utter lack of an opponent. He didn't have wire cutters or the time to find any. He had to pull the wire and hope, or leave it to the experts.

The timer was down to less than ninety seconds.

Jake believed in staying positive. He'd seen

hope affect outcomes, even during military ops. He also placed a great deal of stock in common sense and being prepared. Scrambling back to the nightstand, he retrieved his phone. Taking a picture, he sent it to Brady, just in case they could use it as evidence. Ignoring the rapidly decreasing numbers on the timer, he used the flashlight to see how Driscoll attached the bomb to the bed frame. Two plastic straps held the device in place. He carefully tugged on the straps, but didn't have the right angle or leverage to break them and he'd hidden his knife in the front room. No time to retrieve it.

Desperate, Jake looked for anything to help. He wanted to get out with the evidence to put Driscoll away for good. He didn't want Sloan looking over her shoulder ever again.

"Jake!" Sloan called through the window. "Jake! Where are you?"

"Sloan!" Seth shouted at his sister. "Get back here!"

Jake swore and rolled out from under the bed, bringing his phone along. He couldn't let her get hurt by the blast or another senseless tragedy. They'd find another way to get Driscoll out of her life.

"Move! Move!" he shouted as he ran for the

window. He vaulted through the opening as she and Seth backpedaled. Grabbing her hand, he ran with her away from the house, toward the first responders gathered in the street.

The heat slammed into his bare back a fraction of a second before the sound wave of the explosion. He tucked Sloan into the shelter of his body as the blast knocked them to their knees. Looking back, he saw the bedroom engulfed in flames.

Firefighters rushed to put out the blaze. He noticed paramedics and police surrounding them on the grass. Peering over Sloan's head, he locked gazes with his best friend. As reinforcements went, Seth was the best man to have around. Seth's mouth moved, but the ringing in Jake's ears made it impossible to hear. With a shake of his head, Seth flopped back on the grass.

They were likely being encouraged to move further from the scene, but Jake wasn't ready to move. Wasn't ready to release Sloan. Not even to her brother.

Unfortunately, the first sound he heard was Driscoll. "Sloan! Sloan!"

Ignoring those panicked shrieks, he asked Sloan, "You all right?"

"Yes." Her eyes were round in a pale face

smudged with dirt. In shock, her body trembled against his. "He planted another bomb?"

"Under the bed." He coughed. "A working one. On a timer. Tried to disarm it, move it." His arms banded around her and he pressed his face to her throat. "Ran out of time."

She cupped his face in her hands. "Thank you for not dying."

"Sloan!"

She lifted her head, staring at something behind Jake. Fury lit her gaze, instantly burning away the fear and shock. Slowly, she came to her feet. "You planted a bomb under our bed!"

Jake sat up, unable to control his laughter as he took in the scene. Seth had Driscoll in a hard hold so he couldn't reach them and his eyes went wide as her words sunk in.

Driscoll's mouth opened and closed like a fish out of water as Sloan advanced. "No. Well, yes." His eyes were wide and wild.

"So much for not hurting me!"

"You're in too deep this time," Jake warned. "No escape."

"I didn't arm it until you were out of the house," Driscoll wailed.

That explained a great deal about why the

bastard had been in such a panic when Sloan returned.

On a colorful oath, Sloan punched Driscoll in the stomach. The man doubled over. Or tried to. Seth hauled him upright and she punched him once more.

"This man just tried to kill us," she declared to the nearest police officer.

Jake rolled to his feet, ready to back her up with the pictures on his cell phone, but the police seemed to take her at her word. He wondered how much she'd told them while he was in the bedroom. Working around Seth, they cuffed Driscoll and read him his rights as they escorted him to a patrol car.

Seth pulled his sister into a hug. Then did the same with Jake. Eyeing the two of them, he asked, "Should I assume the worst here?"

Sloan elbowed her brother. "You could assume the best." Pressing to her toes, she kissed his cheek. "Thanks for sending Jake to help."

He raised his hands. "That was all Hank. I respected your wishes."

"Uh-huh." She snorted and scooted closer to Jake.

He put his arm around her, wishing he had

more on than his gym shorts as he faced her brother.

"Take it easy," Seth said. "You've got other priorities right now."

That was true enough. The paramedics insisted on treating the minor wounds on his arm and back. With a blanket over his lap, he sat on the gurney, Sloan tucked beside him.

They had a lot to discuss. Or maybe nothing at all. With Driscoll no longer stalking her, she didn't need a boyfriend, undercover or otherwise. She never had given him a clue about her feelings, if she had any at all for him beyond the obvious. Respect, affection, and phenomenal sex didn't necessarily add up to the long-term forever partnership he longed for.

For Jake, she was the one.

He only hoped she wouldn't be the one who got away.

SLOAN FELT Jake's cell phone vibrating in his pocket. The device was pinched between them on the gurney while the paramedics tended to his wounds. She shifted just enough so he could answer.

"I'm good. Scratched up a little, that's all."

He made it sound like he'd tripped over a rock during a leisurely hike. They'd nearly been blown to bits. She clutched her hands together in her lap to hide the shaking.

The voice on the other end of the call sounded male, and remarkably calm. Had to be Brady. She wished she could make out his words.

"Seriously?" Jake glanced around the scene. "Can't wait to meet him."

In the following silence, Jake reached over, his big hand covering both of hers.

"We're good, Brady. Thanks for the assist. Again. The cops will be happy with whatever you can send." A long pause. "Yes, I will text when we get to the hotel."

"We're not going to my place?" she queried as soon as he pushed his phone back into his pocket.

"No. Brady made a reservation for us. The police plan on searching your home for…"

He didn't need to finish that sentence. She stroked his arm, mindful of the fresh scrapes. "I'm so sorry about Peter."

"Not your fault," he replied. "And it's over now."

She hoped that didn't mean he planned to walk away. Before she summoned the courage to tell him her feelings, to ask him to stay, the paramedics pressed him to go to the hospital.

Naturally, he refused. He hopped off the gurney and held her close as she did the same. She always felt so secure, treasured, when he was close.

"We'll take your car," he said, nudging her in that direction. "Brady arranged for Mike to meet us at the hotel with clean clothes and whatever we need. I think Seth is booked at the same place. So, that'll be fun."

She giggled. Her brother would understand once she explained her feelings. After she told Jake. "Who's Mike?"

"Another Guardian Agency protector. Former SEAL, like Seth. Been with the agency a long time. His wife just had a baby, or he would've been assigned to your case."

She couldn't imagine going through this ordeal with a stranger. It had been embarrassing enough with a friend from her past. "I'm glad it was you." She paused, hugging him tightly.

"Do you trust me?"

"Of course I trust you," she insisted, burrowing closer. His heart pounded in a steady rhythm under her cheek. The sensation did more to steady her than the abundance of first responders, her brother's presence, and help from the invisible Brady.

"Sure about that?" He rubbed his cheek against her hair. "You left me in the bed and went to deal with a treacherous creep on your own."

She looked up, holding his gaze. "You're mad at me."

"A little bit," he admitted.

"Jake, you're *everything* to me. I thought I could talk him out of hurting you or anyone else I love. When I heard how he manipulated those accounts, I knew he wouldn't stop. He would've done anything to hurt us. I was trying to protect *you.*"

"Protection is *my* job." He rested his forehead against hers. "It's right there in the title. I'm a Guardian Agency Protector." His lips brushed across hers. "I get it. You have such a big heart. I love how much you care for others. But you just can't reason with some people. Especially someone bent on murder."

"Clearly." She turned back, watching the firefighters dealing with the mess Peter had made. "I promise I've learned my lesson."

She cuddled close as they walked on. She'd parked near the corner and hadn't been blocked in by the line of emergency vehicles clogging the street in front of the bungalow. Colorful strobe lights crashed through the darkness. Thankfully, they were leaving and wouldn't have to deal with any judgmental or nosy neighbors.

"Well, if I have anything to say about it," Jake said, "this is one lesson we won't be repeating."

We? Wasn't it her lesson to learn? Not that she was eager to be the object of another man's obsessive attention. Unless that man was Jake and the attention was healthy and positive. For a woman so sure she didn't want to try and build a life with a man who would always run toward danger in order to save others, she was irrevocably attached to Jake.

Attached. Ha. She was hopelessly in love. And it was past time she gave him the words. Although he was standing in the street, barefoot, wearing only his gym shorts and a blanket, she refused to waste another minute.

"The other night, on the beach, you said you loved me."

"Still true." He leaned down and nuzzled her ear.

Her hands to his chest, she eased him back. His mouth tilted up on one side and his amusement boosted her courage. "Even though you're mad?"

"Even though," he confirmed. "Your parents have always been an excellent example of what love looks like. Love doesn't change based on conditions."

"I know. It's what I've always hoped to find for myself. Someone steady through the highs and lows and unexpected twists of life."

He took a deep breath, eased back. "You found that with Zach."

"I did, yes." And she'd been lucky enough to be struck by that amazing, life-changing lightning twice.

His gaze hit the pavement, full of trouble and a deep sadness she didn't ever want to see again. She couldn't protect him from everything, but she'd spend the rest of her life trying. If he'd have her.

She caught his hands when he tried to take another step back. "I'd say tonight qualifies as a twist. One we navigated like champs." She linked her hands loosely behind his head. "You were definitely steady. My rock." Gently, she drew his mouth down to hers, kissing him deeply. "I love you, Jake Welch. With every ounce of my body, heart and soul. I love you and I want to build a life with you. A future for us."

"Us." He smoothed a thumb over her cheek. "That's the best thing I've ever heard. I love you so much. Wasn't sure how I was going to walk away." He kissed her again, heedless of the audience. Odds were good with all the first responders milling about, they weren't the main attraction anyway.

"Are you sure?" he pressed. "It's no secret you're not into military guys. Current or former."

"I've said some really dumb things lately," she admitted. "I hope you'll forgive me."

Grief had taken a toll, left some scars on her heart and soul. But she'd grown. Falling in love with Jake had brought a healing she hadn't expected. He'd shown her how much she had left to give. Loving him didn't feel like a risk, it didn't diminish the beauty of the past, only forged something better.

She ran her hands over the warm planes of his bare chest. "You are the perfect man for me, Jake. Let's start working on forever right now."

He opened her car door. As she settled behind

the wheel, he hurried around to the passenger side. "Hotel stat," he said as he buckled his seatbelt.

"What are you doing now?" she asked when he pulled out his phone.

"Ordering champagne," he said. "Strawberries. And a steak. I need to refuel before we celebrate."

Delighted, she laughed as she put the car in gear. She and Jake were building a solid foundation from this point forward. Deep down, she already knew their love would stand through any storm. Reaching over, she laced her fingers with his, reveling in his strength. He'd helped her reclaim her faith in happiness and the healing power of love.

Yes, they had loads to celebrate. First, they'd toast their survival and then they could get a head start on filling all the days ahead of them with joy.

Regan Black, a USA Today and internationally bestselling author, writes award-winning, action-packed romances featuring kick-butt heroines and the sexy heroes who fall in love with them. Raised in the Midwest and California, she and her husband share their empty nest with two adorably arrogant cats in the South Carolina Lowcountry where the rich blend of legend, romance, and history fuels her imagination.

For free reads, exclusive prizes, and much more, subscribe to the monthly newsletter at ReganBlack.com/perks.

Keep up with Regan online:
www.ReganBlack.com
Facebook
Instagram

Or follow Regan at:

BookBub

Amazon

Unknown Identities - Brotherhood Protectors crossover novellas:

Moving Target

Lost Signal

Off The Radar

For full details on all of Regan's books visit ReganBlack.com and

enjoy excerpts from each of her sexy, adrenaline-fueled novels.

Deadly Observations

Deadly Reflections, Behind Closed Doors series

Black Ice, Stormwatch series

what she knew, Book 4 in Breakdown, a multi-author series

Knight Traveler Series

The Matchmaker Series

Escape Club Heroes, Harlequin Romantic Suspense

The Riley Code, Harlequin Romantic Suspense

Colton Family saga, a multi-author series, Harlequin Romantic Suspense

Hot SEAL Salty Dog (SEALs in Paradise)

Hot SEAL Hawaiian Nights (SEALs in Paradise)

Hot SEAL Bachelor Party (SEALs in Paradise)

www.ingramcontent.com/pod-product-compliance
Lightning Source LLC
Chambersburg PA
CBHW070756160726
48004CB00001B/210